the Ghosts we Keep

Mason Deaver

Library of Congress Cataloging-in-Publication Data available

ISBN 978-1-338-59334-1

1 2021

Printed in the U.S.A.   23
First edition, June 2021

Book design by Maeve Norton

for suzanne, my mother,
who first taught me how to heal.

i love you.

I want you to be the very best version of
yourself that you can be.

—marion mcpherson

from the movie *Ladybird*,
written and directed by Greta Gerwig

wednesday, july 3, 2019

after

The summer after my brother was killed, my parents made me get a job at a frozen yogurt shop.

It wasn't that hard to learn how to work things. The hard part was dealing with the customers. Put too few sprinkles on, they complained you were ripping them off. Give them too many, though, and they complained you were only making the froyo heavier to up the price when it was weighed.

Nobody, it seemed, felt they ever had just the right amount of sprinkles.

The shop was downtown, right near the heart of Kinston, and it also happened to be one of the hottest summers on record, so we were never not busy. Sometimes the shop would stay open until eleven, which Mom wasn't in love with.

I didn't mind the job, truly. The uniform was fine; my

coworkers were mostly cool. I liked Julie, who usually shared my shifts. But she was balanced out by one of the managers, Henry, who took frozen yogurt way too seriously. I, however, did not take frozen yogurt seriously at all. The job did what it was meant to do, though. It got me out of the house, and it made me stop thinking about Ethan.

Except when it didn't.

Mom would pick me up after my shift ended. Tonight she'd been waiting in the parking lot for the last twenty minutes, reading her book.

"Bye, Liam!" Julie waved to me as she walked to her car.

I waved back.

"How was your day?" Mom asked me as soon as I got in the car and buckled my seat belt. This question always arrived like clockwork.

She tried to hide the book by throwing it in the back seat, but I knew it was one of those grief counseling books.

"Busy," I told her, handing over a cup of yogurt. We got a free cup once a shift. I always went with basic vanilla, some hot fudge, and those crispy-rice M&M's.

Exactly what Ethan ordered every time we came here.

"Oh yeah?" Mom took a spoonful. She eats the free cups for me because I got tired of eating them two weeks into the job. "That means good tips, though."

"Not always. But tonight was good. Thirty dollars."

"Well, look at that." Mom put the car into reverse and backed out of her spot, frozen yogurt in the cup holder. The drive home was mostly quiet, just the voice of the weatherman talking about a storm coming up this weekend, May showers apparently stretching into the first weeks of July.

Things weren't always this quiet with us. They were getting a little better after our family therapy appointments, but we still hadn't eased back into a routine. Or at least it didn't feel like we had.

Mom didn't really like music anymore. She and Dad used to always have it on, dancing while they cooked, her feet bouncing while she read, his fingers tapping the wheel of the car while we drove.

Now it was the weather on loop.

When we got home, I walked to my bedroom, throwing my froyo-mandatory hat to the back of my closet. I knew that I should shower—I smelled like a cow that had been bathed in vanilla.

I *should've* showered, but now that I was lying in bed, I didn't want to move. My feet hurt, and my hands still felt cold. I stretched my fingers, in and out, trying to get some of the blood flowing through them again.

Then I found my phone.

For a moment I considered texting Joel or Vanessa, telling them how my day had gone; it was muscle memory.

I rolled out of bed, fidgeting to get my shirt off because all of a sudden, the clothes that I was wearing felt too heavy. Even underneath, my skin felt like it was crawling, like it was pressed too tight against my muscles and no matter how I moved my body, everything was too close together.

I wanted to crawl away, to scratch until I didn't feel the itch anymore.

There was a knocking on my door. Dad. "Hey. We're going to bed."

"Night." I threw my shirt toward the hamper in my open closet. I didn't work the next day, so I'd have time to wash it. Hopefully it'd get the vanilla stench out.

I moved out of bed and walked down the hallway to the bathroom, setting the water on the hottest temperature it'd go before I turned on some music and stood in the shower for a bit. Then I took a washcloth and tried to wash the scent of vanilla off my skin. The body wash smelled like coconut and I debated whether or not that was an improvement as I bounced to the beat of the song, humming along to the mess of synths.

I was surprised Mom or Dad didn't knock on the door, telling me to turn down the noise.

I sniffed my wrist and smelled more coconut than vanilla, so I figured that I was clean enough.

Also, I just wanted to go to sleep.

I walked slowly back down the hallway, staring at the door to Ethan's room. Mom and Dad hadn't been in there for a while. They'd begun their summer cleaning out bits and pieces, washing some of the leftover clothes and donating them to Goodwill, but everything else had remained untouched.

Or at least that's what they thought. There were other things missing now, things they'd never known existed.

Back in my room, I turned off the lamp on my nightstand and crawled between my sheets. Every time I closed my eyes, I thought about the yogurt shop. I still smelled the vanilla.

I probably should've been thinking about more important things, like how I was going to get into a good college when I started submitting applications this fall. With everything that had happened, my junior year had fallen apart toward the end. My summer had started with a month of classes.

I'd failed.

The sympathy my teachers felt for me only went so far. Come August, I'd be joining my classmates in our senior year, but all my do-over cards had been forfeited. I was angry with how school had made me handle the entire situation, and even angrier with myself for almost letting everything slip away.

Or perhaps I should have been worried about how I didn't have my oldest friends anymore, and that I didn't know how to get them back.

Or I should've been worried about Mom and Dad. I remembered reading somewhere that 75 percent of marriages end after the death of a child.

But instead of all that, I wanted to worry about the frozen yogurt shop. I wanted to worry about getting my work done before I clocked out, making sure that I got the floors mopped. I wanted to stress out about whether I'd remembered to lay out the toppings for the morning crew. I wanted to be worried about pushing the pumpkin spice flavor because for some reason a dumbass executive had decided that the prime time to sell pumpkin-spice-flavored froyo was July.

I was trying to fool myself, and if the last few months had taught me anything, it was that I was incredibly good at fooling myself. The truth would always find me. No matter how hard I pushed down its ugly head, it would find a way back in.

Always.

And it didn't smell like vanilla.

I still found it so much easier to discuss frozen yogurt instead of my dead brother.

E than died on a Sunday.

The coroner's office told us he was killed between 7:30 p.m. and 7:45 p.m. They couldn't give an exact time.

I was up until four that night (or morning, I guess). Mom and Dad begged me to go to bed, told me to get some rest. They'd already started planning the funeral.

I wanted to shout at them, ask them how they could already be picking out a casket when Ethan's body was only a few miles away at the hospital. Barely cold, alone.

I wanted to be there with him, just so he'd have someone.

He didn't need anyone anymore, though.

My bed was warm, the street now empty where hours ago it'd been lined with cars, all the people who had showed up and started to clean our home for us barely an hour after Ethan died. Consoling Mom and Dad, vacuuming the carpet, dusting the tables, cleaning out the refrigerator of expired food and bringing their own new food.

To this day, I'm still not sure if it's just a southern thing, to take over a family's house when someone dies, or if people everywhere do that.

I blinked, and when I opened my eyes again, it was nine. I felt awful, worse than that time Vanessa and I had stolen some of her dad's whiskey when I was sleeping over. We had wanted to be adults like in the movie we were watching.

I threw up that night and my stomach hurt, and everything felt fuzzy when I woke up the next morning.

Except this time there was no fuzziness, there was no confusion. I knew exactly what'd happened; it was an image burned into the backs of my eyelids any time I dared to close them.

Vanessa.

I rolled over, grabbing my phone and sending a quick text to her, asking her if she could come over. Then I just lay there.

The house was empty once more, as if its very foundation was in mourning.

It was quiet. Until I heard the sound of the lawn mower in the backyard.

For a moment I had hope.

Mowing the lawn was Ethan's job.

Dad and I were both allergic to grass, so the moment that

Ethan could sit in the lawn mower seat and reach the brakes, it was his responsibility. Dad paid him thirty bucks every time he did it.

That was how he'd saved up for his PS4.

I found Mom on the patio, the awning protecting her from the morning sun.

"Good morning," I said, climbing onto the chair next to her.

"Morning," she said, taking a hit off her cigarette. Mom only smoked when she was stressed out, either from school or the heavy hours at work that she had to balance.

This was the first time she'd done it in front of me, as if she wasn't ashamed anymore.

I didn't even think she knew that I knew she smoked.

I almost asked her if I could have one, but I wasn't in the mood for an ass-kicking.

Collecting the ash was that infernal notepad, the yellow paper detailing all the events of the coming week.

"I called your school this morning, told them you'd be absent for a while."

Right, school. I wanted to ask how long *a while* meant, but I had a feeling not even Mom knew the answer to that.

I hadn't been woken up by an alarm this morning. I hadn't needed to race to beat Ethan to the shower so I'd have a few precious ounces of hot water. I hadn't been forced to do anything but lie there, staring at the ugly popcorn detailing that dotted my ceiling, counting the seconds until I had to get up because it was physically hurting to lie there.

I hadn't thought yet about how Ethan dying might disrupt the routine.

I was thinking about it now.

"The whole week?" I asked.

Mom nodded. "We've settled on the funeral being Wednesday."

"Okay."

"You'll need to get your suit refitted," she told me. "It barely fit when Barney died, and you've grown since then."

Barney had been Nana's . . . boyfriend? Husband? You'd think someone in their eighties would feel like dating was a thing they shouldn't be doing anymore, and I never would've called their relationship *romantic*. More like *parasitic*. He'd lived in her house, slept in her bed. They were close on some level, but Nana hadn't even cried for him when he died. That had been the last funeral we'd had to go to.

"Mom, we bought that suit when I was fourteen," I reminded her. "It won't fit me again no matter how much it's hemmed."

"Right." She took a moment to think. "I'll just give you my card, and you can go buy another one." I watched as she took out another cigarette and lit it before speaking again. "Your aunt Donna is coming over."

"I think Vanessa's coming over too," I said.

The night before, as we'd stepped out of Vanessa's car, she'd grabbed me as I fell to the ground. She held me, listened to me cry, rubbed my back, demanded that I squeeze her hand so she knew I could hear her, and attempted to get me to calm my breathing when she thought I was hyperventilating.

"Maybe you two can go ahead and get your suit, get you both out of the house."

"Maybe," I said.

She'd have to drive. I didn't have my license.

"Where's Dad?" I asked, watching as the lawn mower drove by slowly. It was Mr. Dixon from across the street. He was on his own lawn mower too, not our new bright orange one.

"He had to go down to the hospital for something."

"What?"

"I don't know." Mom sounded agitated. "He just had to go. They called him down there."

"But *why*?"

"I don't know, Liam! They just wanted one of us down there and I couldn't . . ." She leaned back in her seat. "I couldn't bring myself to go."

"Okay. Sorry."

Mom didn't say anything; she let me walk back into the house and up to my room with a sick feeling in my stomach. It didn't feel real, even though I'd watched from the side of the road as Ethan was loaded into the ambulance.

I looked at my phone and the first thing I saw was my text to Joel still there, labeled *read* but with no reply.

I guess he had no idea what to do when his best friend texted to say that his older brother was dead.

Vanessa had replied, though.

VANESSA: On my way ♥

After sitting at my desk for twenty minutes, scrolling through all the new *in memoriam* Instagram posts Ethan had been tagged in by his classmates, I got into the shower, just barely bothering to wash my hair and let the water run down my arms and off the tips of my fingers. I couldn't even properly clean myself. I just didn't have the energy.

I couldn't believe it.

I didn't want to believe it.

And yet, the universe didn't care what I wanted. It'd taken Ethan without a trace of guilt or sorrow. Without any pity for what I might feel afterward. I felt it then, the absence of my brother. And I knew that I'd feel it for the rest of my life. In digging for clothes to wear before Vanessa arrived, I found the shirt that I'd been wearing the night before. It was a white shirt, with the words TODAY IS GOING TO BE A GREAT DAY . . . AND HERE'S WHY! from *Dear Evan Hansen*. I'd gotten it the previous year for Christmas, along with a vinyl of the Broadway show that I never dared to actually play because I didn't want it to get warped or worn.

It was one of my favorite shirts. Except now, with new dried red-brown stains, it made me sick to look at, so I balled it up and threw it as far back into my closet as it'd go.

Vanessa ambled up the stairs a few moments later, and we just stared at each other as she leaned in my door frame.

"Hey," she finally said. I stared at her brown skin, the dark circles under her eyes, her curled black hair a little messy, the oversize flannel shirt she wore over her favorite Paramore shirt.

"Hey."

"How'd you sleep?" she asked.

"Barely," I told her.

"You should get some rest," she said.

"Yeah." That was all I could muster.

She sat down at my desk, pressing her fingers on the keys of my keyboard that sat unplugged so no noise came out.

We'd known each other since preschool; she was the first person I'd met on my first day, and she'd joined my protests whenever I'd demanded the teacher finish reading *Where the Wild Things Are* during story time.

We'd never *not* been best friends, but at that moment, I had no idea how to talk to her.

"My mom wants me to go buy a suit," I finally said.

"Yeah . . . I guess you'll need that." She spun in my chair, staring up at the ceiling so that her hair fell back away from her face.

"Will you go with me? I have no idea what I'm doing."

Vanessa's gaze settled on me. "Of course. But what makes you think I have any idea how to pick out a suit?"

"We'll wing it. Plus, you're the one here who has a license."

"And you're the one who could've changed that at any point over the last year!"

"You know I get nervous."

There was just the barest hint of a smile on her face for a brief moment. It was enough to forget everything else for a second. One precious second that felt invaluable.

"Have you heard from Joel?" I asked.

"No, not this morning."

"Did you talk to him last night?"

"Yeah, for a bit."

"Okay . . ." I left it at that. I didn't actually know if I wanted Joel to be with us. It was going to be a long day, and I knew that I was going to be a lot to deal with. I also didn't know if I wanted Joel and Vanessa to hold hands and kiss each other in front of me right now. I only wanted them there to support me.

"Do you want him to come along?" Vanessa asked.

"Nah," I told her.

"Okay then," she murmured.

There was so much I wanted to talk to her about. Joel, Ethan, this new universe that we'd found ourselves a part of. I knew she would've listened, but would she have understood? Would I have been able to articulate how I felt to her when I couldn't fathom understanding myself?

So instead, I followed Vanessa downstairs, and I kept my mouth shut.

Ethan's funeral was a line of people, faces, hands. Some of them I knew. Some of them I'd been in school with since I was in diapers. Some of them were adults who only my parents knew. Some of them none of us knew. But no matter who they were, they all picked phrases out of the rotating pool of things you say at a funeral.

"I'm sorry for your loss."

"I'm so sorry this happened."

"I'm sorry."

"Sorry."

I nodded. I shook their hands. I let them feel like they were helping me. The funeral was late in the day, which meant that an entire section of the church auditorium was dedicated to kids from school. Ethan's teammates served as the ushers, passing out the programs with Ethan's face on them. They'd also be responsible for carrying his casket outside to the hearse. The second, more private part of the funeral would take place at the cemetery, where Ethan would be buried beside my grandfather and my great-grandparents.

I looked down at the flimsy paper in my hand, wet with sweat and worry.

ETHAN DAVID COOPER

1/21/2001—3/24/2019

BELOVED SON, BROTHER, AND FRIEND

The programs were as cheesy as I'd expected. A picture of Ethan from these family portraits we'd taken last year, with a cool blue background, some clouds, and a dove to match.

Ethan would've loved it. He lived for cheesy things like this: bad graphic design or movies that were so awful they were good.

I was thinking this when I felt the tap on my shoulder.

"Hey, do you need anything?" Joel asked. He and his mother were sitting in the row behind my immediate family. I'd heard him whispering to her in quiet Vietnamese through the procession of people.

Vanessa was standing next to me, mostly for extra emotional support. "Lee?" she said when I didn't answer Joel. She rubbed circles in the small of my back, and I couldn't tell if her touch was comforting me or if I was repulsed by the idea of another human being so close.

"Do you have any water?" I asked Joel.

Joel nodded, handing me a bottle that I took several heavy gulps from.

"How are you feeling?" he asked.

"If one more person tells you 'everything happens for a reason,' I'm going to burn this church to the ground," Vanessa murmured.

"Well, Ethan did always say that he wanted to be cremated and not buried," I said, not fully aware of the words that were leaving my mouth.

Vanessa had to hold back a laugh. Joel just stared at me.

"What?" I whispered, careful that my parents, talking to the pastor on my other side, couldn't hear me. "Too soon?"

"I hate you," Vanessa whispered back.

"Liam?"

I glanced over, and Mom was motioning for me to come closer.

"How are you feeling?" she asked. I looked down and saw the balled-up tissue in her hands, stained with black mascara.

"I'm fine," I said, lying.

I didn't tell her that I felt like I was suffocating in my suit, and that I was tired of talking to people, and that one person had called me Ethan and said they were sorry that my brother had died.

I most certainly didn't tell her I was sick of being here, that I just wanted this all to be over so that I could go back home and sleep for the rest of the week.

"I think we're going to cut the visitation line off, get this started," she told me. "I'm ready for all these people to get out of here."

"Me too," Dad added once the pastor was out of earshot.

I looked around at the crowds of people. Ethan was popular. *Very* popular.

What else could you be when you were the star batter on the baseball team and not too shabby at pitching either? Girls fawned over him; boys wanted to be him.

I wondered if these people knew I was Ethan's brother before today.

We looked enough alike. But where Ethan was always in the spotlight, I was invisible. That was the way I preferred it.

From our pew up front, I could turn around and see my class-mates. People who I barely knew, or had maybe talked to a few times. There was Tommy, who I had Earth Science with last year. Melissa and Eric, who were both in my Algebra II class. I was also vaguely aware that Ethan's girlfriend was probably somewhere in this crowd.

I didn't even know her name. Or what she looked like.

I had no idea what his type was. We never talked about things like that.

Now I'd never know.

I looked for Marcus as well, Ethan's best friend since they were four years old. I scanned Ethan's teammates again and again, but I didn't see Marcus anywhere.

The pastor came back to our pew. "Okay, we're going to ask that you all come out with me for the start of the service." He started to walk to the back of the church, Mom and Dad following.

"Should we come?" Joel asked, already halfway out of his seat.

"No, we'll stay here," Vanessa said, moving back a row to sit with Joel. I shuffled away with my nana at my side.

What followed was weird. Not funny-weird or trippy-weird. It was all awful-weird.

There was a lot of standing and sitting, stopping and starting, a lot of staring. We had to move to the back of the congregation and wait as the music started, then head back down to our pews.

And there in front: the closed casket.

Ethan but not Ethan.

As we sat, the pastor walked to his podium. Our church was one of those almost-mega churches. I wasn't even sure what precise religion we were; any time I asked Mom, she just said, "Church of God."

"Today," Pastor Anthony said, his voice echoing through the

speakers, "we are here to mourn the loss of a dear friend to this community. But we are also here to celebrate his life."

I watched as Mom balled her fists together.

"I know that in times like this, when someone so young goes to meet with the Lord, we question His judgment. We ask Him, 'Why, God? Why would you take such a new life? Someone with everything ahead of him?'"

I wanted to hit the pastor.

I wanted to march up to the stage and break his jaw.

"In first Thessalonians four, verses thirteen and fourteen, the good word says, 'Brothers and sisters, we do not want you to be uninformed about those who sleep in death, so that you do not grieve like the rest of mankind—'"

I couldn't believe the words I was hearing, I couldn't believe I was watching the pastor of this entire congregation turn my brother's funeral into a generic sermon. The pastor wasn't talking about Ethan.

He didn't know Ethan at all.

"Shut up, shut up, shut up," I muttered under my breath. I felt Dad lay his hand across mine, taking it tightly in a grip that helped drag me back up to the surface. I just needed to ignore the pastor, to shut out his words. That was easier said than done, though. I felt relief as he reached the end of his testimony, but then I realized there was still so much of the funeral left.

Ethan's baseball coach, Coach Tanner, came up to the stage,

where he proceeded to stare at me and my family on and off for the ten minutes he talked.

"I've never known a kinder soul, someone more willing to help out his fellow man than Ethan. He was loved by this team, by these students . . ." He stopped and started several times, barely containing himself before he'd slip back into the soft tears that men were rarely allowed to have in front of other people. "He was one of the best players we'd ever had, will ever have. And I know that he's going to be missed—"

I listened to these words and tried to pair them with my image of Ethan. Yes, he was nice, he was kind. But these people never knew the side of him that I knew, the side that came with being someone's sibling and sharing the same space with them for sixteen whole years. The fighting, the spitting, the punches. The late nights talking, the days of ignoring each other because we'd said something that we'd later regretted.

Ethan's coach didn't know the story of the time Ethan and I played hide-and-seek, and how when I tried to open the door to the bathroom where I *knew* he was hiding, he pushed it open quickly, forcing the doorknob to give me a black eye that lasted for a month. Or the time I had the TV remote and wouldn't give it up, so Ethan just sat on top of me until I started crying.

All three of us had been asked if we wanted to speak during the funeral, but we'd all said no. I didn't know Mom and Dad's reasoning, but I guessed it was the same as mine. What would

I even say? How would I get my thoughts onto a piece of paper and read them to hundreds of people? So there was no one to recount these stories of the real Ethan, the Ethan I knew—but simply thinking about them made me feel better.

When the funeral was over, the last songs sung, the music swelled again and the guys from the baseball team marched up to the front of the chapel to get Ethan ready.

His casket was kept closed because the scars and marks left all over his face were too much for them to cover with makeup.

That was what I'd figured anyway.

I wouldn't have wanted anyone else to see Ethan the way he was. The day before, we'd been able to view the body at the funeral home. His skin was blue and red—the burns on his skin from how hard he hit the asphalt, the bruises that had formed on his face, the angle of his nose because it was broken.

They'd told us that he hadn't felt any pain.

It had been instant. There was no suffering.

I couldn't believe that.

There was always suffering.

The ride back home was silent between Mom, Dad, and me. And as we pulled into the driveway, the house didn't feel the same. For the last two days there had been the line of cars up and down the street; some people had even parked on the shoulder of the road where Ethan had been hit. I knew that it couldn't be safe or legal for people to park there, but they did it anyway.

I climbed up the stairs, my tie already hanging loose around my neck. I was in the process of unbuttoning my shirt when I walked into my room, sliding it all off in one swoop and leaving it on the bed, before I heard Dad's words echoing in my head to hang it back up so that it wouldn't wrinkle. As much as I didn't want to, I took the time to slip the suit back into the garment bag and left it in my closet.

And then it was all over.

The funeral was done, my suit was packed away; it was time to move on.

My phone buzzed in my hand.

VANESSA: do you want us to come over?

I took *us* to mean her and Joel because of course it did.

The idea of being around people at that moment made my stomach roll.

ME: No, you don't have to.
ME: I'd rather be alone.
VANESSA: Okay, let me know if you want us.
ME: Thanks.

It wasn't like they could do anything; they'd sit there, ask me how I was feeling, and I wouldn't have an answer for them because I didn't know, but that wouldn't be the answer they wanted. It wouldn't be the right answer, even if it was the honest one. I didn't know how I was feeling; I couldn't feel anything except numbness. Simple, reliable concepts like time moving forward, or even the space around me, didn't feel real. It felt more like a dream that I'd wake up from soon.

But it wasn't a dream.

And I wouldn't wake up.

Mom knocked lightly on my door frame. "Hey."

"Hey," I said from the spot under the sheets where I'd crawled to protect myself from the world.

"How are you feeling?"

My favorite question.

"You know." I tried to sit up a little bit, but I didn't want to give too much away. I hadn't changed into anything, so I was sitting there in my underwear, and I didn't want Mom to see all that, even if she'd seen it all before.

"Yeah," Mom said. "Are you hungry?"

"Not really."

"Have you eaten anything today?"

I shook my head.

"Eat something, okay? Even if it's just a snack."

I opened my mouth to answer with an *okay*, but Mom was one step ahead of me.

"And don't just say 'okay' and not do anything. Please actually eat something."

"I will," I promised.

"Thank you." She gave me a slight smile, and then it was silence for a few awkward moments before she nodded and walked away. Even talking with my mother felt abnormal now.

We'd lost the normal. How could we have a normal anymore?

I didn't know what to feel. I wanted to scream until my voice was raw and my throat bled. I wanted to cry because I hadn't cried since I'd seen Ethan on the road, blood pooling underneath his body. I willed myself to let the tears come, but they were locked behind a door that I didn't have the key to.

You have to breathe slowly, in and out, okay? Vanessa had told me this after we saw his body, when she'd gotten me home. Her dad was an EMT, so she'd learned the basics after being forced to sit through class after class when he couldn't find a babysitter. *You're going to pass out. I want you to match my breathing.*

She'd placed my hand on her chest, and I'd tried as best I could to match the rise and fall.

I remembered how everything had hurt, how it hadn't seemed real then either. Our neighbors had come out in droves, staring at the police cars and the ambulance, the reflection of the red-and-blue lights as they broke into the darkness of the night.

I remembered how every second had felt like an eternity, how it had felt like the night was never going to end, and how I wanted to be able to press rewind on the universe, back to when things were normal.

But it was real life, and there was no undoing what had happened.

"Come on, Ethan! Let's get it!" Dad called out from the bleachers.

Our home team, the Devils, was down by two points, and it was the ninth inning. All Ethan had to do was hit this one out of the park and the game would be ours. We'd been doing so well all season; a win here would only cement the Devils' standing as the championship approached and would also boost Ethan's chances when it came to scholarships.

But the Hawks were good.

Really good.

Ethan was up at bat, and he already had one strike against him. Coach Tanner stood on the sidelines, watching closely, as Ethan's teammates in the dugout cheered him on.

"Let's go, Cooper, you got this!"

"Come on, Cooper!"

"Ethan! Let's do this, dude!"

I watched Ethan focus. I'd been watching him long enough to know his tells. I could see the grip on his bat was too tight, his stance a little too wide.

He was stressed out.

Worried.

If only he knew that he had this, that he'd swing and the ball would soar through the air and we'd score those three points we needed, securing our win and ending the game.

Which was exactly what he did.

Ethan watched as the ball soared into the air above, slowing his steps as if he knew he could take his time with this one.

The crowd erupted.

We cheered, we screamed. Once Ethan crossed home plate, the Devils stuck in the dugout ran out onto the field and lifted him into the air. Marcus was right there, carrying Ethan on his shoulders. The Hawks all hung their heads in shame.

Eventually, the celebration calmed down enough for both teams to line up and do the honorary handshake ("Good game") before the Hawks skulked away.

The Devils all kept talking, gathering their equipment, marching back toward the locker room so they could shower and get ready for whatever the rest of the day held for them. I already knew that Ethan and Marcus were going to a party; there was always a party after these huge games.

"You did good, son." Dad wrapped his arm around Ethan's shoulders. At sixteen, he'd already sprouted above Dad.

"We did it." Ethan was grinning from ear to ear.

"*You* did it." Dad pulled Ethan down to his level, rubbing his knuckles along the top of Ethan's head.

Ethan shook himself free, flattening down the sweaty hair that hung in his face. "I'm going to go shower. You guys can wait for me in the car."

"Okay. You still going over to Rodger's tonight?" Dad asked.

"Yeah, probably. Is that cool?"

Dad smiled. "After that game you played, you can do whatever you want."

I tried to not let that bother me. The last time I'd asked to hang out with Joel and Vanessa, I'd been told no. It hadn't even been a school night. And we had Easter lunch at Nana's the very next day, and we all knew that Ethan would stay up way too late, get home early in the morning, and be impossible to wake up.

But he still got to go?

All because he played a good game of baseball?

Once Ethan was gone, Dad said, "Come on, Lee. Let's go wait in the truck."

We sat there, and we sat there, and we sat there. We had a

perfect view of the gym from the parking lot, so we could count as each of the boys from the team made their way out to their families.

After half an hour of waiting, Dad flagged down the next boy who walked out.

"Hey, Keith, you see Ethan in the locker room?"

"Um . . ." Keith looked around. He had long curly hair that hugged the back of his neck, and I'd be lying if I said that I hadn't thought of him some nights. My face flooded red any time I saw him at one of these games, especially in his baseball pants. I knew what my obsessive curiosity meant, but I still hadn't really admitted it to myself. I told myself I just liked the pants, that's all.

"Nah. Last I saw him he was still out by the field." Keith brushed the hair out of his face and I had to look away. "He might've gone back for his glove—probably forgot it in all the excitement."

"Okay. Thanks."

"No problem." He tapped the roof of the truck and walked away.

"Do you want me to go find him?" I asked.

"Yeah." Dad looked around, as if Ethan would materialize out of nowhere.

"Okay." I unbuckled my seat belt and climbed out of the truck, walking across the parking lot.

I marched through the grass, toward the field. I spotted him in the dugout, sitting on the bench.

It didn't look like he was searching for his glove.

Before I could make it to him to ask what was going on, I saw another person was there with him.

Marcus.

I kept walking, watching the two of them as Marcus sat down next to Ethan and they started to talk.

A lot of the time it felt like Marcus was a second brother to me. He and Ethan always hung out together after school, pretending to fight in the living room or arguing about what to watch on television. When I was younger, I was desperate to impress Marcus. He always seemed like the cooler guy between the two of them. Marcus had the new toys and video games and was lucky enough to be an only child. He was usually a dick to me. Not in a mean way, just an older-kid kind of way.

In the last two years or so, I'd found myself crushing on Marcus—without actually saying the words out loud to myself. I knew what they meant; I didn't need the explanation. I liked the way his hair looked, and his smile. I loved the way he gave me attention, even when he was picking on me. He'd usually let me join in on whatever he and Ethan were doing, even when it was obvious that Ethan didn't want me there.

I wasn't stupid. I knew that Marcus wasn't gay. I'd heard rumors about him in middle school, about him being the first boy to lose his virginity, and how he seemed to have a new girl-friend every few weeks.

I inched closer, neither of them realizing I was there; they just kept talking. Nothing else, nothing interesting. Marcus leaned in so that he was facing Ethan, and he handed him something. I couldn't tell what it was. I could just tell it was important from the way Marcus held it, and the way Ethan smiled as he received it.

Then he looked up and saw me.

"Liam? What are you doing?" Ethan asked.

He didn't sound happy to see me. Whatever the moment with Marcus had contained, I'd ruined it.

"Dad, um . . . Dad wanted me to come and get you."

"Okay."

Marcus grinned from ear to ear, taking Ethan under his arm and pulling him close. "Everybody wants a piece of the champ. Only fair."

"Hey! Stop!"

I noticed the baseball in Ethan's hand. I immediately figured it was the one he'd hit the home run with, the winning ball. What else could it be? Marcus must've gone searching beyond the outfield to retrieve it for him. Which felt like such a Marcus thing to do. Always trying so hard to be the Boy Scout.

"We were just talking," Marcus said, still squeezing Ethan tight. "Why don't you tell your dad Ethan will be there in a bit, okay?"

"Okay." I took another glance at the two of them. Marcus's smile was so infectious that Ethan couldn't help but catch it.

He was unguarded in his happiness, clutching the ball that maybe, just maybe, had taken him one step closer to a future made out of major league championships and trading cards.

I never got to see him that way. So I took it in a couple of seconds longer before returning to the parking lot.

"Where is he?" Dad asked when I got back to the truck. I took my opportunity to sit in the front seat, to claim that prize from Ethan. He'd probably fight me for it, and Dad would tell us to stop fighting and me to get into the back seat. Because Ethan had earned it, or whatever.

"He's coming."

Dad turned the volume on the radio a little louder, and I tapped my fingers to the country song playing. I always liked it better when he chose the oldies station over the country one. It didn't take much for me to get tired of songs about tractors and drinking and girls. Especially when I lacked an interest in all three topics.

Ethan came back ten minutes later, looking happier than I'd ever seen him. He didn't even say a word about me being in the front seat; he just climbed straight into the back seat, buckling his seat belt, the ball sitting right beside him.

"Everything okay, son?" Dad asked.

"Yeah, everything's great, Dad."

"I asked your brother to go check on you." Dad put the car in reverse and started to pull out of the parking spot. "But clearly you're doing just fine."

"I am," Ethan said. And then he said it again, like he couldn't believe it himself. "I really am."

I'd always wondered what the connection between food and funerals is. Whenever someone died, you had to go to their home, and you had to give them food.

Too much food.

And then, for the next week . . . more food.

And more food.

And *I promise we're just stopping by to drop this off, also how are you doing, how are you processing this recent trauma,* more food. Enough food that there's never any hope of a home with only three people ever finishing it. So what isn't eaten is either thrown away or left in the large white freezer out in the garage.

And that's exactly what happened with all the food people gave us after Ethan's funeral. So much food that we had to load it all into my mom's car and drive it over to my grandmother's house. Apparently Nana had wanted everyone who was already in town for the funeral to stop by, so I think Mom figured this was a good chance to get some of her fridge space back.

"Oh, hello, sweetie." Nana was the first person to greet me at the door. She would've wrapped me in a hug if it wasn't for the pan of cold macaroni and cheese I was carrying.

"Hey, Nana," I said, letting her kiss my cheek before I moved to the kitchen.

"Look at him, such a handsome boy!" she said to my mom, who was coming up behind me.

I shot Mom a glance. She'd tried to have a talk with her about how my pronouns were *he/him* and *they/them*. *I* knew I certainly wasn't a boy or a man, but it'd never really sunk in with Nana. Not that I'd expected it to. Nana was old, set in her ways, and she forgot things.

Constantly.

I just tried to brush it off.

Nana's house was one of those places that were a constant in my life. Ethan and I both used to stay here a lot when we were younger, less and less with every passing year. Over the last year and a half, we'd mostly only visited for holidays and the seasonal birthday celebrations we had four times a year because this side of our family had grown so big.

It should have been a comfortable familiarity, but right then, it felt like a jarring familiarity. I didn't want to be in the house with its old creaking furniture, the television blasting some local newscast because Nana couldn't hear, with no Wi-Fi or cell signal to save me from the chronic boredom that came with being here for hours on end.

I tried to remind myself that I liked my grandma and enjoyed being around some of my family.

Aunt Donna was in the kitchen, sifting through the food that Mom and Dad had already dropped off. "Hey there, sweetheart," she said when I walked in. "Do you know how much more is left?"

I shrugged. "We loaded up the trunk."

"Okay." The frustration in her tone was obvious. "I'll get the oven preheated."

Aunt Donna was a lot like Mom. As Nana had gotten older, they'd both become her caretakers. They were the ones in charge of holiday dinners now, of coming over a day before the festivities to get everything ready, of answering her phone calls to hear about some second cousin's aunt who was twice removed from the family and nodding along to the story being told without context.

"Who all is coming over?" I asked.

"Everyone who could. Carrie even got in from Washington last night. She was sad she missed the funeral, so she wanted to stop by."

Carrie was my second cousin . . . I thought. It was hard to keep track in our extended family.

"She missed quite the party," I said. Then I turned to Ethan to share a look, only to be struck with the realization.

Aunt Donna stared at me, that earnest look in her eyes. "How are you doing?"

The only reply I could muster was: "I'm doing."

"Your mother—is she . . . ?"

"Is she what?"

Aunt Donna chuckled, but not in a happy way. It was more in a way that told me she was tired, worried. "I was going to ask if she was okay, but I already know the answer to that."

"Yeah, it's about what you'd expect."

I hadn't told anyone what I'd heard the night before. I'd walked down to the kitchen to get a glass of water, and as I crept down the stairs, I saw the blue light shining from the archway that led into the living room. Three stairs up from the floor, I could narrowly peek around the corner to see Mom on the couch, watching reruns of some sitcom on TBS while she cried silently.

I'd wanted to go down to her, to make sure that she wasn't alone. But I couldn't bring myself to do it. I suppose I wasn't strong enough to see her like that.

To see her that broken.

*   *   *

As the family get-together stretched on, more people arrived. My great-uncles and great-aunts, first and second cousins, a friend of my grandmother's who I'd never met but who insisted that she knew me when I was a baby.

Aunt Donna and Mom reheated more and more food, and people came through to grab plates, taking it into the dining room or standing in the kitchen to nibble. I made myself a plate of reheated Bojangles' chicken but only picked at it.

Even though I knew I should eat, I simply didn't have an appetite, and any food that I did manage to eat only turned sour in my mouth.

I sat there in the den, the only room with a television, as one of my older cousins flipped between watching the UNC game and a NASCAR race, spouting out terms I vaguely understood.

Without a word, I stood up, weaving between the kitchen and the dining room, eventually to the living room, where most of the people were gathered. I saw Nana on the couch, tissue in hand, while one of her friends comforted her.

I stepped outside, through the garage.

Mom caught my eye. "Hey, sweetie." I wasn't sure when she'd moved outside, but she stood with Aunt Donna, a cigarette in one hand. Something told me that Dad didn't know about this.

"Hey."

"What's the situation inside?" Aunt Donna asked.

"The guys are watching the game. Nana is in the living room crying."

Mom let out a sigh, then took a long drag. "So the usual."

"The usual," Aunt Donna agreed.

I left them to their talking, making my way over to this large tree that'd been alive longer than my grandparents and parents combined. It stretched above the house and was always a concern during hurricane season because of how close it was to the garage. I found the swing that hung from one of the branches, the rough rope scratching the palm of my hand before I sat down and kicked my legs off the ground.

I pulled out my phone and my earbuds, scrolling through Spotify for too long before I settled on the self-titled album by Mura Masa. A text message appeared along the top of my screen.

VANESSA: so I have this new song.

VANESSA: would you listen to it???

ME: Sure, send it.

A little gray box with an eighth note appeared under her previous messages, and I hit play.

Where Vanessa and I typically preferred to make loud, experimental noises with our keyboards and software, this was just her on the guitar, strumming along to an invisible beat playing inside her head. There were no vocals yet, and she was typically the lyricist between the two of us. When I was having trouble, I always went to her.

ME: When did you write this?

VANESSA: been working on it on and off for a week or two.

VANESSA: do you like it???

ME: I do!

VANESSA: really?

VANESSA: you aren't just saying that?

ME: I promise.

ME: It sounds like a love song.

VANESSA: huh i guess it does.

ME: It's quiet.

ME: I like it.

VANESSA: where are you today?

ME: My grandmother's house, family gathering because of . . . well . . . you know.

VANESSA: yikes . . . i'm sorry.

ME: Yeah . . .

"Liam, sweetie!"

I looked up to see my aunt Donna waving in my direction.

"Come inside. Nana wants to see you."

"Oh boy," I muttered under my breath. Again, I felt the impulse to look to Ethan, to pull him in with me so we could deal with this together. Something told me this instinct would take longer than a few days to get over.

As soon as I got to the living room, Nana said, "Oh, Liam. Sweetheart, would you do me a favor?"

I faked a smile for her sake. "Sure, Nana. What's up?" I had to raise my voice for her and make sure I looked at her while I talked so she could read my lips. Despite having been fitted with hearing aids, she never liked wearing them.

Nana had her own ideas, like most people her age seemed to.

"Would you play the piano for Ruby?" She looked to her friend who was still sitting on the couch. Ruby smiled at me, her eyes looking enlarged through her Coke-bottle glasses. "Oh please, I was telling her all about how you're so good at it. You'll play, won't you?"

"Sure, Nana," I told her, and the rest of my surrounding family started to applaud me, as if I'd done something special.

I never liked playing in front of them. I always felt the pressure, and traditional piano wasn't my style anyway. Sure, I'd had years of lessons, of memorizing songs and notes and keys. But some of the songs I knew weren't ones that I'd want to share with my family. (I doubted that Ruby would want to hear a piano rendition of Charli XCX's "Vroom Vroom.")

There were easy enough songs I could use to impress everyone, "Für Elise" being one of them. I relished in the way it stretched my fingers and made me balance from one end of the piano to the other.

I sat down at the ancient piano, one that had been here since I was a child, just like everything else in the house. It sounded crass, but the older I seemed to get, and the more I realized that my grandmother's time on this Earth was coming to an end, I occasionally wondered if she'd ever leave the piano to me.

Something to remember her by, something to play during my empty moments.

Ethan had never even touched a piano. One Christmas he'd wanted a drum set, and because of my "music expertise," Mom and Dad had asked for my advice. When I sat them down and showed them just how loud drums were, they put an end to that. Ethan wasn't even that upset, and he'd gotten over his newfound dream in mere hours. I'd offered to teach Ethan about the piano, or tell Mom and Dad about drum pads, but he was over it as quickly as he'd gotten interested.

I pressed the foot pedals in time with the music, allowing my hands to flow freely. My fingers danced carefully with the ivory, one hand keeping the solemn background of the song while my other hand battled out the larger sounds, the balance back and forth. I looked up at Mom sitting next to me, and Dad standing above her.

The rest of my family smiled as they watched me play, and Nana came over, resting most of her body along the rear of the instrument, watching me.

I watched the keys. I listened to the music as I created it.

For a moment, I forgot all about Ethan.

Then the song was over, and the mourning returned.

Even though I was surrounded by my family, I realized I'd never felt more alone.

G od, this sucks."

Ethan leaned over the back of the piano, not quite looking at me. In fact, I wasn't even sure if he knew who he was talking to. But there was no one else around.

"What does?" I asked.

"This funeral," he told me, looking around at all our family gathered together once again. It'd been a few months since we'd gotten together to celebrate the summer birthdays.

"We didn't even like Barney," Ethan continued.

"But he was married to Nana," I said. "Or at least I think he was?"

"I have no idea. I mean, look at the way he treated her. She always talked about how he was getting angry in his old age and cursing at her."

I shrugged, hitting a few of the keys together.

The piano needed a tune-up. I seriously doubted it'd ever been cared for in the proper way. I would've loved to pick it apart, have a good look at the guts inside, and see if I could make it sound better. Of course I wouldn't have known where to begin with that process. The lessons Mom and Dad paid for only covered what to do with the keys.

At least it could still be played, and Ethan was right, this funeral was kind of bullshit.

"She liked having him around."

"Yeah, well . . . I always thought it was weird. Besides, Nana has had enough husbands in her lifetime; she shouldn't be dating at her age."

Could you even call it dating? We sure as hell never did.

"I can't argue with you there." I slowly drew my fingers away from the keys. "She doesn't even seem that beat up over it."

"She's more upset that he died in her bed. She was complaining about how she'll have to go to JCPenney to buy new sheets."

I laughed, shaking my head, because our grandmother truly only knew of two places to shop: the JCPenney in the nearly abandoned mall down the street and the Piggly Wiggly around the corner. She could get everything she needed at those two places.

"That sounds exactly like her," I said.

"And now she's pulled out the photo albums and is going through all of them."

"Ah, photo album time." I never missed that. "Who did she grab this time?"

"Luke and Carrie."

"Yikes. They're going to regret coming in from Washington."

"Well, they missed Christmas and Thanksgiving last year, so if they skipped one more family event, they'd never hear the end of it."

Nana was big on family, and you only ever got a certain amount of chances, even if you were directly related to her.

"What were you playing?" Ethan asked me.

"Hmm?"

"The piano?" He pointed to my fingers, his tone indicating that he was wondering if I was stupid or not. "What song were you just playing?"

"Oh, nothing. Just fooling around with it." I closed the keylid.

"You know, you never let me hear your music. You won't even give me your SpaceCloud account."

"*Sound*Cloud," I corrected him. "And that's because it's bad."

"Please," Ethan scoffed.

I knew most of my music was bad; it was unrefined and I was copying nearly every popular producer instead of making things up on my own. The worst part was that the songs weren't even good copies. I had a fraction of their talent and equipment, so I did what I could manage. I was young, I had time, but I also still felt like I needed to prove myself, to have something out there already. If I didn't, I was a failure.

"Play another song; I never hear you play anymore. You've always got on those headphones."

"E—"

"No, I want to hear you play." Then he looked around. "Besides, it'll save me from having to talk to Greg about baseball."

"Fine." I lifted the keylid once again, placing my fingers gently on the keys, trying to figure out what song I could play. I didn't know many versions of more modern songs; my old piano teacher always wanted me to focus on Beethoven, Chopin, Debussy, Tchaikovsky.

I'd watched some YouTube videos and practiced them myself. I knew some FKA twigs and Gaga. Billie Eilish, Twice, and Red Velvet.

I didn't want to play any of that for Ethan, though.

I didn't know what I wanted to play.

So I closed my eyes and let my fingers do whatever they wanted to. I let my mind wander, let the music fill the space between the two of us. I never liked showing Ethan my music because he was so uninterested. The one time he'd ever attended a piano recital of mine, one of the few I was forced to do as a child, he'd simply told me that I'd done okay at the end of it.

I didn't think of it as funny until a few years later, when I realized that he had no right to judge. He wasn't the one playing the instrument; he didn't play any instruments, for that matter. All he knew how to do was swing a bat and run around a dirt field.

Ethan seemed to be enjoying the music now, though. His eyes were closed, and he was weaving back and forth, almost as if I were playing a lullaby that was pulling him into sleep.

"I liked that," he told me after the last echoes of the final notes I'd played had vanished into thin air.

"Thanks."

"Do you think you're going to make music? Like as a career or whatever?"

"I don't know. It's not an easy way to make money."

That, and I was unsure of what my role would be in that world. Would I want to stay behind the scenes, produce and write the music that other people would be famous for singing? Or would I want to be in the spotlight, have it be my name on the tickets and the songs?

"I think you should," Ethan told me. "Fuck money."

"Well, okay then." I laughed, playing a few notes again. "Mom and Dad probably won't like that. I think they think this is just some hobby, or they're holding out hope I'll join a symphony or something."

"You're going to let them tell you what to do?"

I'd never expected Ethan of all people to ask me something like that.

I didn't say anything; I just stared at the keys silently.

"I'm serious, Lee. Don't let them force you into some kind of box. You should do what you want to do."

I could hear the sadness in his voice, the melancholy, as if he were giving a warning rather than a piece of advice.

We sat there for a beat while I played more notes, a quiet echo, a slight sourness to them because the piano had been neglected for so many years now. I stretched to the far end of the piano, my suffocating suit pulling at the space along my side and underneath my armpit. I hit the final note, C7.

The piano was so out of tune that it merely created a sharp intake of breath before letting go.

"Are you doing what you want to do?" I asked Ethan.

"Yeah," he told me. "I am."

after

I lay in bed, knowing that, in the morning, I'd be going back to school.

Both Mom and Dad told me that I didn't have to go back if I wasn't ready. They said they'd do whatever it took, talk to whoever they needed to, in order for me to be excused from classes.

I was ready to go back. I needed to be out of the house. I needed to be away from these walls, from Mom and Dad, from Ethan. And I figured that going back to school would help that.

Help make things normal again.

But I couldn't sleep.

I tossed and I turned, staring at my ceiling. I'd get too hot and kick my blankets off, then I'd get too cold and have to drape them over my body again. I rolled over, turned my pillow around to get at the cool side, but nothing seemed to work.

I watched videos on my phone, scrolled through Instagram and Twitter. But my feed was still being flooded with pictures of Ethan.

Gonna miss you man. @EthanCooper01

can't believe you're gone, I want you back friend. @EthanCooper01

You're gone, but you'll never be forgotten @EthanCooper01

All the pictures are of Ethan with his friends, these people who seemed too cool or too old for me to hang out with, not that he would've ever let his kid sibling hang out with his friends anyway.

I lay there for longer than I knew, before it felt like the shadows along my walls were creeping too close to me. Someone drove by outside, their headlights shining through my window for the briefest of moments. Our road was never that busy, not unless traffic was backed up along the highway, forcing people to cut through our neighborhood to save time.

We didn't even have sidewalks.

I had to get out of that house.

I slipped on my sweatpants and a hoodie, lacing together

my shoes before I untangled the headphones in my pocket and started playing my favorite Big Thief album.

I didn't know where I was going. In fact, there really wasn't anywhere I could go. Vanessa and Joel lived too far away to walk, and I didn't have my license, and it would be years before Kinston even thought of getting Uber or Lyft.

So there was nowhere.

Nowhere that I belonged.

That didn't matter, though; I just wanted to walk. I just wanted to breathe.

I reached the end of our short driveway, looking left and then right. There were no headlights, and the only streetlights visible were those that people had constructed themselves, added to their own yards.

The moon led my way.

I turned right, just like Ethan had.

I walked until I saw that familiar spot, where I'd seen my brother's body. Even in the darkness I could see the orange X, the one that lord-knew-who had painted on the street to mark where Ethan had landed.

In my fit of confusion and exhaustion, I decided that the shoulder of the road was a fine place to sit, the early morning dew soaking my butt through my sweatpants.

I just wanted to sit here.

This was enough.

I could feel it.

I was unsure what sitting here accomplished for me, but the idea that I was still close to Ethan on some level was good enough for me. He was here, his spirit, something he'd left behind. I'd never truly believed in ghosts or whatever, and the jury was still out on whether I believed in a god or some higher almighty being that was watching over me, determining everything that I did or said. I liked to think that there was, but I never knew for sure.

After a few minutes, I spied headlights coming from the opposite end of the street, inching closer and closer. I couldn't tell if they saw me.

Is this what Ethan felt? I asked myself. *Did he know the car was coming? Could he hear it coming from behind? Was the mortician right; was there truly no suffering? Or did he lie there, halted by the pain, unable to breathe as the blood filled his lungs, wondering where we were? Why we weren't there to save him. Why I wasn't there.*

I sat there, watching the stars above my head, these dead things that hung in the night air, light-years away, already gone. I waited for answers that wouldn't come to me.

Then I noticed the cross.

It stood on the other side of the street, a crudely made white wooden cross, dug into the ground. The closer I got, the more details I could make out. The fake flowers left to the side, the pictures, Ethan's name written on the wood like this was his actual gravesite. I felt so many emotions at once. Anger, frustration, hatred, sadness, loneliness. I wanted to destroy something, and I also wanted to cry. I touched the cross, which came up to my thighs, running my fingers along the wood until I felt the sharp sting of a splinter as it punctured the tip of my finger.

It hurt, but I could finally feel something beyond my own emotions. This was physical; it wasn't a mysterious release of chemicals in my brain. This was a real thing, a reminder.

I took one last look at the cross, then walked away. Back down the street, back through our garage, back to my room.

At some point, I actually fell asleep.

In my own bed, not on the side of the road. I was stupid, but not that stupid. I felt awful; my head was hot and my chest was heavy. I almost wondered for a moment if this was what a heart attack felt like.

Could a sixteen-year-old even have a heart attack?

Surely there had to be cases.

I resigned myself to research it later as I hit the snooze button on my phone one more time.

"Liam?" Mom pushed my door open slowly.

I had my eyes closed so I didn't see her, but my door always had a familiar creak to it. Every time Dad said he'd fix it, he'd forget moments later.

"Mhmm?" I mumbled.

"Time to wake up." She paused. "Are you still going back to school today?"

Was I?

I could just say no, stay home all day, get some more sleep, avoid all my classmates, all the pathetic stares and the comments, the people wondering how I was doing because they hadn't moved on yet, the people who just wanted to make sure that I was okay.

"I'm going," I mumbled into my pillow.

"Okay, well, go ahead and get up. Your dad or I will take you."

"All right." I rolled over.

I showered, pulling the handle for the water almost as hot as it'd go. I stared at the splinter in my finger, finally able to see it. When I was done showering, I spent far too long wrestling with tweezers to get it out. I dressed in this oversize sweater that I could pull the sleeves down around my hands and my favorite pair of black jeans.

If I was going to go to school today, I was at least going to be comfortable.

"You ready?" Mom came to my door again thirty minutes

later. I hadn't done anything to my hair, so it was sticking up at the ends, but that was okay.

"Yep."

"Okay, let's go. We're already running late." Mom was dressed like she had somewhere to be after she dropped me off, but I didn't ask what she was planning.

She took the long way around again, avoiding the place where Ethan had died. We drove along the two-lane street until we came to the highway that would lead us right to East Lenoir, passing by the tobacco and cornfields that populated the spaces around the campus.

Mom drove all the way down the street and turned around at the dead-end cul-de-sac so she could get out easier.

"You're sure you want to go today?" Mom reached for me, brushing my hair away from my ears. "I could talk to your principal. Maybe we could get you a few extra days?"

"Yeah, it'll be fine."

I stared at the front door of the school, at my classmates who were hanging out around the entrance because they wanted to spend every possible moment before the bell outside the place they'd be trapped for the following eight hours.

"Okay, I love you." She leaned in to kiss my forehead, and I didn't pull away.

"You too." I grabbed my backpack, shutting the door behind me as I crossed the street, making sure that the coast was clear before I started up toward the front lawn to the main entrance of the school. I passed by some kids; some of them spared a glance at me, others ignored me. This one girl in a black shirt glared at me the entire time I walked up the wet grass toward the flagpoles that represented both America and the great state of North Carolina.

When I walked into the front hall of the school, I weighed two options in my head. I could go find Joel and Vanessa, talk to them, see how they were doing. Or I could stay on my own and go to the hallway near the student center where lots of kids hung out in the morning before first period. Some time to myself might be nice, but so would seeing my friends.

I'd missed them.

I hadn't seen either of them since the funeral, which didn't make me feel great. Maybe they were just giving me my space, but that wasn't what I'd wanted.

None of us had texted the group chat in days except to pass along funeral and visitation information. I *really* wanted to see Vanessa; I wanted to talk to my best friend.

I decided, then began walking slowly toward the cafeteria, bracing myself for the stares of my classmates. I'd imagined the scenario in my head, and it was the exact reason why I'd wanted to avoid the cafeteria at all costs. I'd open the doors and the entire room would go silent; people would stare at me, or run up and start crying, telling me how sorry they were. Everyone would have to get their turn and I'd just sit there, slowly wanting to sink into the linoleum-tiled floor.

That wasn't what happened, though.

I opened the doors, and there were a few looks my way, but everyone stayed in their seats, eating from small plastic cartons of cereal or picking apart English muffins that looked drier than a pile of sand.

Joel and Vanessa were in our usual spot, in the corner of the cafeteria near the door that led out to the senior eating area. We usually walked out that way after lunch to get to fourth period easier.

"Hey." I marched right up, dropping my backpack on the table and taking my seat across from them.

"You look exhausted," Joel said. He took small bites off his unfrosted blueberry Pop-Tart—unfrosted because those were his favorites and he hated frosting on most—if not all—pastries. Vanessa and I couldn't understand it.

I looked at the both of them. They'd so clearly been enjoying each other's company before I'd arrived, and now they'd have to deal with me. They didn't say that, but I could see the expressions on their faces.

I shrugged, looking around the cafeteria. A few faces were sparing glances my way and then turning back to their friends and tablemates.

"I'm here," I said.

"That's the equivalent of 'please kill me,'" Vanessa replied.

"Yeah, well . . . that's about where I am."

"Liam—" Joel's finger pointed to someone behind me.

I turned and saw Melissa Kennedy staring at me. I also noticed the shirt that she was wearing. It was dark blue with white font, the colors of the school, with the words RIP ETHAN COOPER, GONE BUT NOT FORGOTTEN over her heart.

I wanted to vomit.

"Hey, Liam," she said with a smile, as if there was nothing wrong with this situation. I didn't hate Melissa—we'd been in classes together since elementary school, the curse of living in such a rural area. But we'd never been friends.

She went on. "I wanted to see how you were doing."

"Oh, I'm . . . fine, I guess."

"Are you sure? Because I know what you've been through."

I knew enough about Melissa to know that wasn't true at all.

"Yeah . . ."

"I just wanted to check on you."

"Yeah."

"You know"—she lowered her voice—"we were all so heart-broken when Principal Elmore called everyone into the gym to tell us what happened. I started crying."

"Yeah."

As far as I knew, Ethan and Melissa weren't friends either.

"We all did, we were so sad."

"Um . . . thanks, I guess."

"We designed these T-shirts," she said, turning around so I could see the back. A picture of Ethan, one that looked like it was ripped right from his Instagram account, was a block on the back of the fabric, with his name and the dates written underneath. A feat in graphic design.

"Oh . . . nice," I said, because I didn't know what the hell else I was supposed to say to that.

"My mom is selling them, donating the profits to the school."

"Oh." I looked at her. "Did she ask my parents' permission?"

Melissa looked confused. "Why would she?"

That was when Vanessa stepped in. "'Cause, you know, Ethan was *their son*."

"Oh, I mean like . . . yeah, right? You'd think," Melissa sputtered.

"And they could maybe use that money to pay for the funeral expenses?" Vanessa pushed.

"Yeah, but the school needs that money for the sports teams and stuff, you know?"

"The money from cutting the music program last year wasn't enough?" I asked, quickly growing tired and angry with this conversation.

Melissa forced a laugh and smacked my shoulder. "You're so funny."

"Oh yeah, a laugh riot. This whole conversation is *so* funny,"

Vanessa deadpanned, and I had to stop myself from snorting in front of Melissa.

"Anyway, would you guys be interested in shirts? I can give my mom your size, have it done tomorrow? Liam, you wouldn't have to pay for one, it'd be the least we could do. Vanessa and Joel, it's only thirty dollars."

"Wow, what a deal," I said, my voice flat.

Melissa just stared at me, as if she believed I was actually considering if I wanted an overpriced shirt with my dead brother's face to wear around.

"Um, I think I'll pass," I told her.

Her smile vanished. "I'll just tell my mom you thought about it, okay?"

"Yeah, sure." I tried my best to communicate that this conversation was over.

"We're not interested in any shirts," Vanessa said. "Only in your complete lack of shame."

"Okay. Bye, Liam!"

As Melissa darted away, I slumped in my seat, turning back toward the two of them.

"And as quickly as she appeared—" Joel began.

Vanessa finished for him, waving her hands around as if she were casting a spell. "She vanishes."

"That was actually unbelievable," Joel said.

"What?"

"That whole thing! What she just did. Didn't it make you angry?"

"I mean . . ." I looked back over toward Melissa, where she was now seated with her friends, continuing their conversation. A few of them had matching shirts as well, the other suckers I'd guessed Melissa's mom had roped in. "Yeah, it doesn't make me feel great."

"Then you should've told her to stop it," Vanessa told me.

I shrugged. "It's whatever."

"It's not whatever."

"I just . . . I don't want to start something, okay?" I looked at both of them. "Please."

Vanessa's shoulders sank. "Okay. Whatever you say." She didn't sound pleased.

"So what else did I miss?" I asked them, mostly in a desperate attempt to get the conversation away from my complete lack of a backbone.

"Well, firstly. I'm glad you're back—it was so boring without you here to pester," Joel said with a grin, wiping away the pale crumbs from the corners of his mouth. And his words actually did their job, since I did feel a little lighter knowing that he'd missed me.

He went on. "I mean, nothing super weird happened. You heard from the source, Ol' Elmore had an assembly Monday morning to, um . . . give everyone the news. Stuff was rough for a few days after that. Michael Bell cheated on Joanie, so people were talking about that. And in one of Tyler Clay's Snapchats people swore you could see one of his testicles. He took it down, but everyone was already spreading screenshots."

"So what was the consensus?" I asked.

"Oh, you could totally see testicle," Vanessa said.

"Really?" Joel eyed her.

"What? I just wanted to see." Vanessa slumped her shoulders. "You also missed a quiz in geography."

"Right, I forgot about that," I said.

"You missed a lot of work."

"Yeah, I know." My teachers had been good about emailing my assignments. But in the last one I was sent, there was a note that I needed to go and see the guidance counselor once I was back on campus. I was already dreading going to the office, but I figured that I might as well get it over with. Didn't want to have to waste my precious lunch period talking to Principal Elmore or my teachers.

"I'll see you in English," I told Vanessa.

I waved bye to Joel and walked out of the cafeteria, some people still staring at me. I wondered what they were thinking as they saw me, if they already knew who I was, or if their friends were telling them that I was the little brother of the boy who'd died two weeks ago.

I pushed through the glass doors that separated the central

hallway and the cafeteria. Our school was a mishmash of different styles. Our cafeteria was very sleek and modern looking, with those walls that were mostly made of glass and let in all the natural light you could need. But past those doors, the hallways were ugly tan bricks, repainted every other year or so. There were ancient-looking lockers, and there was a faded mural painted on the floor near the entrance. A complete clusterfuck of architectural design and integrity.

"Well, hello, Liam," Mrs. Wilcock said from behind the desk of the front office.

"Hi, Mrs. Wilcock." I leaned over the front desk, which looked more like a kitchen counter, complete with a marble top.

"How are you doing, sweetheart?"

"I'm okay, I guess." I didn't know what else to tell her. I wasn't going to tell the receptionist at my high school that I was depressed and it felt like I was trying to crawl out of quicksand.

"I was so sorry to hear about your brother. What a kind soul."

"Yeah, I was told I had to sign back in after my absences and make sure everything was in order. I have the note from my parents," I told her abruptly, not wanting this conversation to continue any further.

"Ah," she said with a smile full of pity. "I'll be right back."

"Okay." I looked at the pale blue walls, the ticking clock, the pictures and pieces of paper that were pinned to corkboards, the sign-in sheet for guests, the chairs that people had to sit in while they waited for whoever they had to talk to.

I watched as Mrs. Wilcock disappeared down the hallway. When she came back two minutes later, she was with Mr. Kelly, one of the three guidance counselors we had at the school.

"Hi there . . . Liam, right?"

"Yes, sir." I eyed him warily. "Is something going on?"

"Oh, no, I'm just glad you came right to the office. Saves us the trouble of calling you in."

"What trouble?" I asked.

"No trouble! I just wanted to talk to you. Would you join me in my office?"

"Won't I be late for class?"

"I'll be sure to give you a note." There was a tone to Mr. Kelly's voice, one that told me that I didn't really have a choice about whether or not I went to his office. He wanted to talk, and I was going to have to listen.

Mr. Kelly's office was a normal office.

Posters telling me not to give up, plants that looked like they hadn't been watered since school started, and a computer with a fan that was spinning far too loudly.

"Take a seat." He motioned to the two faux leather chairs in front of his desk as he sat in his own spinning desk chair.

I sat down, and he waited.

And waited.

And waited.

I didn't know where he wanted me to go with this. I mean, I *knew*, but that didn't mean I wanted to discuss it with him.

I understood that it was his job as a counselor or whatever, but I just wasn't feeling up to it.

"So, I'm sure you know why I wanted to talk to you."

I nodded.

"I can't imagine what you have gone through over these last two weeks. I just wanted to extend a hand out to you. I am your counselor, after all." He let out this weak laugh while I remained straight-faced.

He should have said something funny if he'd wanted me to laugh.

"I just wanted to make sure that you knew if you needed to talk to someone. Anyone at all. That I'm here."

"Thanks, Mr. Kelly."

I knew that nodding and saying thank you would be the fastest route to escaping this office, getting to class.

"Okay . . ." Mr. Kelly said, as if he was more prepared to have a makeshift therapy session now rather than later. He reached into his desk, pulling out a small hall pass for me. "I also wanted to let you know that some of your homework you missed can be considered optional when it comes to your grades. You have quizzes you'll need to make up, but you can do that at your own pace. The last thing we want is to overwhelm you with schoolwork."

At least this visit had brought some good news.

Mr. Kelly clicked his pen, wrote my name down, signed his own at the bottom, and handed me the pass.

"Thanks again, Mr. Kelly."

"Of course. I just wanted to speak with you, Liam. I hope that was okay."

"Um . . . sure," I said, trying to hide the uneasiness in my voice.

"About Ethan."

I'd really thought we were done. But now I could see that he'd kept a hand on the hall pass, effectively making me his hostage.

"I just wanted to make sure that you're processing everything, that things are okay at home?"

"I mean, they're not," I told him.

Maybe he expected a different answer, but his expression went from one of concern to surprise.

"I'm sorry to hear that."

"Yep." I hung my head, not wanting to meet his gaze. "I'm, um . . . I'm going to miss first period, Mr. Kelly, so if it's okay—"

"Oh, of course." He stood up quickly, and I took that as my

sign to grab my things. "I just wanted to make sure you were doing well. Not that you should feel pressure to *do well*. You know what I mean."

"Yeah, thanks." I could taste the sourness in my mouth, the bile rising up.

"Well, Liam . . . just keep in mind that we all miss him."

I nodded, wanting this to end.

"And that everything happens for a reason, even if we don't believe so."

"Thanks, Mr. Kelly." I did not wait for his reply; I simply opened the door and let it slam behind me as I walked out of the office, my hall pass forgotten on Mr. Kelly's desk.

That was quite all right because I wasn't going to class. Instead I went to the bathroom, the one that was next to the empty cafeteria. I picked the handicapped stall so I would have more than enough room to empty the contents of my stomach into the toilet. It was mostly water, clear, but the bile still stung my mouth, made it burn in an unfamiliar way.

Everything happens for a reason.

Everything happens for a reason.

Everything happens for a reason.

I thought of those words, my stomach lurching once again as I rested my head against the pale blue brick wall, littered with messages of someone claiming to have slept with a friend's mother and phone numbers promising a good time if called.

In any other circumstances I would've felt revolted at myself for even daring to touch anything in this bathroom. But in that moment the tiled floor came as a relief to my fevered hands.

I tried to keep my mouth closed as I cried, shoving the sleeve of my sweater in my mouth, feeling as it went cold with my own saliva, the tears streaming down my cheeks.

I just wanted him back.

I wanted him back more than anything I'd ever wanted before.

I wanted to go back in time, to stop him from going for his daily run, to go back and beg him to stay inside so he wouldn't be hit by a car that would leave him to bleed out on the asphalt.

I wanted my brother back.

The door to the bathroom swung open, which was odd to me because people only used this bathroom when they were in the cafeteria.

I kept myself quiet, sitting in the filth of the bathroom, waiting for this mysterious person to leave.

Then I heard the crying.

It was a shriek at first, the kind of sound I imagine an animal caught in a trap would make, screeching out in pain and begging for whoever was hunting it to put it out of its misery. The sink ran, but I still heard another sob, and another. And sniffling.

I stood slowly, sure that the sound of the running water would mask the sound of my sneakers against the floor, and I peeked through the crack in the stall door.

It was Marcus.

Marcus, staring red faced in the mirror, his eyes just as red and rubbed raw.

What is he doing? I wondered.

Perhaps I should have left him alone; maybe that would have made things easier. But instead I flushed the toilet and unlocked the door, watching his reflection as he wondered who had heard him crying, then the realization that it was me in here with him.

"Marcus . . ."

He turned quickly, wiping under his eyes.

"Liam—what are you doing here?"

"I was . . ." I looked back at the stall, all evidence of my fit flushed down the drain. "Yeah."

"Yeah?"

"Are you okay?" I asked. A stupid question. I already knew the answer.

He was probably as far away from okay as I was.

But I still asked because I didn't know what else to do.

"Yeah, I'm fine."

"You weren't at the funeral," I said.

He turned back to the mirror, cupping his hands under the water and scrubbing at his face.

"Can you leave, Liam? I need some time alone."

"I was here first," I said.

Marcus's reflection stared at me. "Please, just leave."

I didn't want to because I didn't know where else I could possibly go. But I left anyway. I left Marcus to be alone because if he couldn't give me what I wanted, then I was going to give him what he wanted.

What I wanted was to talk to him, to ask how he was handling everything, to see if he wanted to come over, see Ethan's room, maybe take something to remember his best friend by.

It didn't seem like the right moment.

Then again, when would there ever be a right moment to invite someone to grieve, to mourn?

There was no right moment for any of it.

I hid in the bathroom.

I didn't know where else to go. East Lenoir was such a big school, way bigger than my middle school was. There were so many hallways, so many more students, and all my classes felt like they were miles away from one another.

I didn't want to do this.

I wanted to go home.

I'd already formulated the plan in my head. I'd survive the rest of today, and then when I was home, I'd beg Mom to home-school me. All she had to do was her own homework since her classes were online; she could teach me, she had plenty of time.

Joel and Vanessa would probably be disappointed, but that was whatever. I couldn't be at this school for another moment.

It was already hard enough not calling Mom then and there, begging her to come and pick me up.

I'd felt strange all day, walking around the campus as if I was supposed to know where I was going.

During freshman orientation, Dad and Ethan had walked my path with me, Ethan giving me all the shortcuts to get to my classes faster.

But I hadn't been fast enough for Mr. Perkins, my Algebra II teacher.

I'd missed the bell because I'd had to go to the bathroom before first period, and I'd gotten lost because it wasn't a part of my path. He'd slammed the door while I was just a few feet away.

"I told you my rule at the start of the semester, Mr. Cooper," he'd told me with the door to the classroom barely cracked. "I would be lenient on your first two days here, but not another day more."

"Please, Mr. Perkins, I just got lost. I swear I didn't do it on purpose."

"Think of this as a learning exercise. Now report to the office for detention."

The words made my blood run cold. The last time I'd gotten in trouble I was in kindergarten, and all I'd gotten was a red piece of paper by my name on the board.

"Please, Mr. Perkins, I didn't mean to be late, I swear."

And looking past him, I could see every single one of my classmates; some people I'd known since elementary school, others that were faces entirely new to me. They were all staring, so relieved they hadn't been the one on the other side of this door.

"Mr. Cooper, I don't care if you didn't mean to be late. I was very clear on your first day that after yesterday you would either be on time to class or you wouldn't be allowed inside. If I break the rule for you, I must break the rule for everyone else. Which I won't do."

"But I—"

"Report to the office. Now."

He'd closed the door in front of me and even went so far as to draw the blinds when I didn't move right away.

I didn't want to cry, but I could feel my eyes getting hot, the familiar ache in my jaw that meant tears were coming. So I ran toward the cafeteria, toward the bathrooms that I knew were there.

I hid inside the last stall, not caring what would happen.

Though that didn't keep me from thinking about it.

Mr. Perkins would hear that I'd never reported for ISS and he'd be furious, I'd be called to the office and probably suspended for real, forced to stay at home all week while Mom and Dad yelled at me for being late.

All on my third day of high school.

Now I was stuck in a bathroom, unsure of where to go or what to do. I could've called Mom, but that seemed disastrous. Dad was more easygoing, but he still wouldn't be happy to hear that I was skipping class.

Ethan?

Would he care?

He had gym first period, which meant they'd either be out in the field or maybe in the weight room, so he probably wouldn't have his phone with him.

But maybe I could find him?

I wiped my eyes and blew my nose on some paper towel that felt as if it were made of sandpaper, then walked across the campus to the gym, silently praying that no teachers would pop their heads out of their classrooms and wonder where I was going.

For all they knew, I was on my way to the office, or to ISS like I was supposed to be.

I walked through the sterile white halls as they blended into sections of the school that had yet to be renovated, the same halls that my mother walked through twenty years ago when she was a student here. Past empty lockers because hardly anyone at this school actually used them, past posters for clubs and teams, upcoming games and events at the school.

A quick peek into the weight room told me it was empty, so I walked to the track, the one that wrapped its way around the football field. I strolled past the concession stand, through the entrance to the bleachers, keeping myself hidden from Coach Tanner's gaze.

Though he knew I was Ethan's brother, and he adored Ethan, so I doubted that he'd actually care that I was here.

Ethan, Marcus, and the rest of the boys in PE this period were all doing laps around the track. I watched them silently as they ran around. It was so hot that many of the boys had chosen to do their exercises without their shirts on, their sweat-covered bodies shining in the heavy morning sunlight. I didn't want to watch them too closely, but my eyes were drawn to them, the way their chests heaved with air, the way their muscles flexed and relaxed as they ran as fast as they could. Attempting to beat one another in a race that didn't matter, one that had no consequences.

I gripped the metal railing of the bleachers as I felt the front of my pants grow tighter, trying my best to ignore the pit in my stomach. That's when Marcus saw me. He stopped slowly, his momentum going too strong for him to simply halt his sprint. He had to let it go, had to give his legs the room to slow.

But when he did, he headed over to where I was hidden, checking to see that Coach Tanner wasn't looking.

"Lee?" Marcus was one of the boys who'd decided to keep his shirt on . . . though the tank top was made of such a thin fabric that there wasn't much of one there. I could clearly see what was underneath, even if it made me feel ashamed. This was my brother's best friend; I shouldn't be thinking about him this way . . . and yet, I couldn't help myself.

"What are you doing?" he asked.

"Can you get Ethan?" I asked him, my eyes threatening to water again.

Marcus must've noticed, or simply didn't want to deal with his best friend's kid brother by himself. So he raced off, looping around the track and catching up with Ethan. In the middle of their sprints, Marcus pointed over to me and communicated all that he needed to. As they both came closer, they slowed down, maneuvering their way onto the bleachers.

"Lee, what's going on?" Ethan asked me.

He was just as sweaty as Marcus, with his hair plastered to his forehead.

"I . . ." I started to say, but now that I needed to, I couldn't get the words out, as if they outright refused. "I was late," I told him.

"Late?" Marcus stared at me, this bewildered look on his face.

"What, for class?" Ethan asked.

I nodded.

"Okay?"

"Mr. Perkins wouldn't let me into class." I started to cry, feeling that weight on my chest. "He told me to go to ISS. I didn't know what to do. I just got lost, I didn't mean to be late, I didn't know where I was going, and I—"

"Hey, hey." Ethan looked around, looking unsure of how to deal with his sobbing little brother. "Come on, let's go somewhere else."

Ethan led me by the shoulders, closer to the far side of the concession stand, which stood in hidden view from the track area.

"Don't cry about it," Marcus told me.

"I'm sorry." I wiped my eyes with my hands.

"Why did you come out here?" Marcus asked. "Why didn't you just go to ISS? Ms. Holland is actually pretty chill."

"I didn't want to get in trouble," I said.

"Well, skipping ISS is probably going to get you into more trouble," Marcus pointed out.

"What?" I managed before I started to cry again. Through the tears I could see Ethan smack Marcus on the arm.

"He's kidding, Lee." Ethan took a seat beside me. "It's okay; it's not a big deal."

"Mr. Perkins was just such an asshole."

That made Marcus laugh, and then Ethan chuckled too.

"Yeah, he is." Ethan wrapped his arm around my shoulders. "It's okay, though. There's no reason to cry. It's not that big a deal."

"But Marcus said I'm going to get in trouble."

Ethan sucked on his teeth. "You're not. Mr. Perkins is some power-hungry jerk. He just wants to make you feel bad. He's not actually going to check to see if you reported."

"Really?"

"Yeah." Ethan looked at Marcus.

"Oh, yeah," Marcus said quickly. "Right. He gave me ISS like five times when I had his class and never checked up. I even skipped the last three times I was supposed to go."

"So you're good—you hear me?" Ethan said.

I wiped my eyes, nodding too quickly. "Yeah."

"Okay." Ethan patted me on the back before he stood up, stretching his legs. "We've got to get back to the track before Coach notices we aren't there anymore."

"Where do I go?" I asked both of them.

"Well . . . you can stay out here," Ethan said.

"Coach will see when he comes to sneak his cigarettes," Marcus warned.

Ethan looked at me, and then back toward the field. "Fine . . . this way, Lee."

"Where are we going?"

"Secret spot," Ethan told me, a wild grin on his face.

We walked past the bleachers, around this fence, getting closer and closer to the baseball field with each step. Both Marcus and Ethan were able to hoist themselves over the fence in one swift movement. I, however, had to hook my feet through the openings of the five-foot-tall fence and climb my way over it carefully. They kept leading me, around the edge, through the clay-colored dirt, to the home-team dugout.

"Why here?"

"It faces away from the school," Marcus said. "Only time it gets used is during a game."

Stepping inside, there was an immediate temperature change. The air felt thick, but the fenced opening allowed the breeze to blow in. There was nowhere to sit except an uncomfortable-looking metal bench that seemed like it'd bruise me if I sat there for too long.

"Just hide here until your next class," Ethan said.

"What are you two going to do?" I asked, setting my backpack down.

"We've got to go back," Ethan told me, because of course they couldn't just skip the rest of the period to hang out with me.

I doubted they'd want to do that, even if they could.

"Right."

"Just start heading over before the next bell rings and you should make it to class on time," Ethan advised.

"How do y'all know to come here?" I asked, my hands tracing along the cement block wall that was adorned with a mural depicting the school's team name in big graffitied letters.

"We skip class sometimes," Ethan said, and then Marcus shot him a look that told me he didn't want me to have that information.

"Dude."

"What? Sorry!" Ethan said defensively. "He asked a question."

82

"I won't tell anyone," I said.

"Good." Ethan pointed a finger at me. "Just relax here. Don't draw attention to yourself. No one should see you anyway."

"I won't. I promise." I sat down on the bench, watching as Marcus and Ethan both moved slowly toward the opening that would carry them back to the field.

Ethan was already halfway out the entrance when he turned back to me. "And, Lee?"

"Yeah?"

"Don't be late again. Mr. Perkins is a tough SOB."

"I won't." I watched Ethan and Marcus leave, and listened to their footsteps as they sprinted towards the track field as if nothing had happened.

I stayed there for the rest of the hour that first period lasted. I stayed inside this quiet escape from the world, this box that seemed to be cut off from any existence outside it. No one knew that I was here, and that allowed me to watch and wait.

tuesday, april 9, 2019

after

It shocked me how little time it took for everyone at school to go back to normal. Of course, I didn't know what that first day was like for everyone, or those weeks I was gone for that matter, but things seemed normal again already, for everyone except me.

I had gone back to class after my meltdown, but I hadn't been able to focus on anything my teachers were saying. I'd kept thinking about Marcus, about why he'd been crying. Was he really sad after all? He hadn't showed up to the funeral . . . but had that been because he couldn't handle the stress of seeing his best friend buried?

I hadn't been able to stop thinking about it, spiraling down while I buried my head on my desk. A few of my teachers might have wanted to tell me to pay attention, to sit up and do my assignments like it was a normal day, but I was milking that whole dead-brother thing, so even if they'd wanted to say something, they hadn't.

On my second day back, Vanessa ran up to match my stride in the hallway, keeping her books clutched close to her chest. "Hey," she said, "do you want to come over after school? I want to work on this song with you."

"Oh yeah?"

"Yeah, so, don't tell Joel because I want it to be a surprise. It's a song for our anniversary." She was whispering now, and my heart began to sink. As much as I loved both of them, I didn't want the reminder that they were so deeply in love with each other and I was completely alone, left to be the third wheel.

"That's cool," I told her, trying my best to feign enthusiasm, but that only made me feel more like a dick.

"And, um . . ." Vanessa stalled, so I slowed my pace. "I'm also going to try to release an EP before the end of the year?"

"What?"

"Yeah, I've got it all planned out too. Five songs. I'm working on ideas for the album art, but I don't know what I want it to be yet. But yeah . . . I want to do it!"

"Holy shit—that's amazing!"

Vanessa beamed at me, so proud of herself. "I want your help with it."

"What do you mean?"

"Well, you know I'm ass at the piano, so I was hoping you wouldn't mind collaborating on parts with me, maybe with a producer credit?"

For a second I pictured a world where Vanessa's music went viral or got noticed by a huge production company because it was just that good. And then people would see my name on the producer credits, hear my tag in the song, and Vanessa and I would both get attention, get signed, get to work with musicians.

It wouldn't happen like that at all. But it was nice to imagine for a second.

"Yeah, I . . ."

"What?"

"I can't do it tonight," I told her.

"Something planned already?" Vanessa laughed. We both knew that she and Joel were the only people I ever had plans with. If I wasn't with them, I was most likely lying in bed, goofing around in GarageBand or watching music tutorials on YouTube. I didn't have a life outside of them, and it would've made me angry if it hadn't been so true.

"Family stuff," I lied.

"Okay, that's cool. How are your parents?"

To my ears, it sounded like she was asking more out of obligation than actual concern.

I shrugged, unsure of what to tell her. "I mean, how well

off can they be? It's been two weeks." I tried not to let my tone betray my words. I wasn't angry at Vanessa.

"Yeah," Vanessa muttered, her voice gone quiet.

"The police are still trying to find out what they can about the car that hit him."

"Oh, that's awful."

"The people who saw Ethan get hit said it was a green SUV, but they don't remember the license plate number. They couldn't even begin to guess the year."

"I . . ." Vanessa shook her head. "Fuck."

"Yeah."

Vanessa didn't say anything after that, which was fair—I wouldn't have known what to say either. But something would've been nice. Perhaps it was my fault for discussing it, for bringing it up.

I always felt that she and Joel were sick of me talking about my problems—and that was before I had a problem like this.

Mom was quiet on the drive home from school that day.

She'd texted me in the middle of the day to let me know that she'd be picking me up, and that I didn't have to ask Joel or Vanessa for a ride. I took the text to mean that she hadn't gone back to work.

I wondered when she would.

I'd gone back to school; Dad had gone back to work.

Maybe going back to work would help her forget, help her work things out?

"How was school?" she asked as I buckled my seat belt.

"Fine. Good." I adjusted the strap against my chest. "Boring."

"That's . . . good?"

"Yeah, I guess." I watched out the window as she pulled out of the parking lot. When we got home, Mom settled at the dinner table, turning on *Dr. Phil* for the afternoon.

For a moment I considered talking to her, asking her about the episode at Nana's, or if she was doing okay, even though I knew she wasn't. I just wanted to talk to her, to break down this wall that'd been built between us without our permission.

Instead I walked up the steps to my room, stopping in front of Ethan's room to stare at his door, wondering if Mom and Dad had taken the time to go through his things like they said they planned to. My hand reached out, as if commanded by some invisible force instead of my own mind, and I wrapped it around the door handle.

The door wasn't locked; it hadn't been nailed shut; there was nothing in the universe keeping me from opening it. So I did.

Just a crack, just enough to see inside.

His room hadn't changed at all yet. The tan walls were decorated with a few posters of baseball players I never would've known the names of if they weren't also on the poster, a few pictures of us as a family, his television against the far wall, the hardly used desk, the unmade bed, his closet door hanging open so I could see his shirts and jackets. Mom and Dad hadn't touched anything. This was Ethan's world, the world that he'd left behind. I walked in, over to his bedside table, and found a textbook for school, the keys to his car, and a baseball that I recognized well. I picked it up slowly, turning it over in my hand, fingers tracing the red stitching.

Then I put it back, left everything in its dead place.

I closed the door and kept walking to my own room, making a choice between working on music or crawling under the sheets because I felt like I could sleep for a hundred years. Vanessa's words had struck a chord within me, and if she was going to work on music that she wanted to show the world, then I wanted to do the same thing.

Was that petty? Perhaps.

Was I being an asshole? Lying to Vanessa that I was busy and couldn't help her with music, just to work on my own private projects?

I was feeling a little bitter about it earlier, when it seemed that she didn't care about what was actually going on with me and my parents and Ethan. As if I had to beg her forgiveness for wanting to talk about my brother, who'd been dead for two whole weeks.

I sat down in my desk chair and opened the last song that I'd been working on. I'd stolen the lyrics from Charli XCX's

"Unlock It" and had tried to invent a new beat to go underneath it.

That was how I found most of my ideas: taking vocals from a singer I liked, overlaying them with something new, seeing what fit and what didn't. By the time I was done, the song sounded completely different . . . though I always tried to keep a piece of the original song in there somewhere, as an homage, a treat, if only just for me.

As I listened back to my own version of "Unlock It," I hated everything I'd done. It all sounded messy, without purpose.

I couldn't bring myself to scrap it entirely; I'd worked on it for far too long. But the more I listened to it, the less I actually wanted to work.

I even dragged out my keyboard, trying a few different chords to see if I could salvage anything out of this song. I ended up slamming my hands down on the keys, producing a loud screeching in my headphones.

"Lee?"

I hadn't even seen Dad standing in my doorway.

"Oh, hey, Dad." I slipped my headphones off, leaving them dangling from my neck. "When did you get home?"

"A few hours ago."

I looked at the clock in the corner of my computer screen, and sure enough, it was steadily approaching seven o'clock. Guess I'd gotten too into the song to notice the time.

"Dinner's ready," Dad told me in an exhausted voice. "We've been calling you for ten minutes."

"Sorry. I was busy."

"Yeah, well." He waited, motioning toward the stairs. "Come on, your mother is hungry."

"Okay."

I left my headphones hanging off the monitor and grabbed my phone, slipping it into the pocket of my hoodie. The smell of dinner wafted up the stairs, and from the landing I could tell that it was Dad's roast chicken. I silently hoped that he'd prepared his seared asparagus to go along with it, maybe some potatoes too.

For the first time in days my stomach growled and my mouth watered as I sat down at the dinner table.

"Nice of you to join us," Mom said directly.

I wasn't sure if I was meant to read her tone as a joke or something serious.

"Sorry, I was working on this song."

"Hmm." Mom took her seat, and then Dad.

I grabbed my fork and knife and cut into the juicy chicken, salivating at the way my imagination almost allowed me to taste it before I'd taken even a single bite.

The silverware clinked against the ceramic of the plate. When I cut through the chicken, I put a little too much force behind it, and my knife nearly slid right through, screeching along the plate, sending a chill down my spine.

"Sorry," I whispered as Mom and Dad both looked at me.

Mom gave me a slight smile and went back to her food.

"This is really good, Dad," I said, biting off a piece of asparagus.

"Thanks, Lee."

"Yeah, really fantastic, honey." Mom chewed a piece of chicken, and Dad nodded at her in approval.

Glasses were picked up and set down, mouths were wiped with napkins, feet tapped along the floor. A car drove by outside, the wind rustled the tree that grew next to the house. I cleared my throat; Mom sniffled.

This was the soundtrack of our house in mourning. There was no room for conversation. No one wanted to know anything about one another right now; we just wanted to eat in silence and not have to think about Ethan on anyone's terms but our own.

When I was finished, I didn't ask for seconds, even though I was hungry enough to devour another plate. Without a word, I took my dishes to the sink, rinsed them off, slid them into the dishwasher, then raced back up the stairs to my bedroom.

I attempted to get into my musical groove, sliding my headphones back on, but after ten minutes or so, I couldn't stand the sound of what I was working on. So I threw the headphones down, grabbed the copy of *Macbeth* from my backpack, and tried to get my school reading done.

I didn't want to think about what Mom and Dad might've been doing downstairs. They could've been talking about me, they could've been completely frozen in time, they could've been fighting. But because I no longer saw them, they no longer existed. For a few hours, I was allowed to be alone with no one but myself.

And that was how I preferred it.

W hat are you two doing?" I asked Ethan and Marcus as I marched into the living room. They were seated close together, a bowl of popcorn between them.

It was obvious what was going on; the movie was playing on the TV. But I still wanted to ask anyway.

"Watching a movie," Ethan said.

"What movie?"

Again, an obvious question, considering the way that LEGO Batman was bouncing around the screen, cracking jokes while Robin followed him.

"*The LEGO Batman Movie*," Ethan said.

"Isn't this a little-kid movie?" I asked, sitting down on the armchair next to the couch.

"*LEGO Batman* is a true classic for all ages," Marcus said.

"You know," Ethan told me, "you don't have to watch it if you don't want to."

"I'll watch," I said.

"Didn't you have some homework you wanted to finish?" he asked. "Or a song or something."

"No," I told him.

Ethan let out a long sigh, then whispered something to Marcus.

"Whatever." I kicked my legs over the arm of the chair and settled in to watch the rest of the movie. I sat there for the remaining hour, watching Batman and Robin and Batgirl kick ass, fighting the Joker and Harley Quinn. I also had this perfect view of Marcus and Ethan whispering, laughing, two best friends who wanted to hang out and watch a movie.

I wanted to watch the movie. And if I got the chance to be closer to Marcus and watch him out of the corner of my eye . . . well, that was just a plus.

He stood up as the credits started to play, and Ethan followed him.

"I should get going," Marcus said.

Ethan whispered something so I couldn't hear, and then Marcus replied, "Nah, I'll text you when I get home." They both walked out toward the garage and I called out a goodbye to Marcus, but I was a few seconds too late, delayed by my self-consciousness. I sat there wondering why it mattered so much to me that Marcus noticed me, that he wanted to be my friend too and didn't just think of me as Ethan's little sibling. A few minutes later, I could see his truck pulling out of the driveway. Ethan strolled back into the house, heading right to his spot on the couch.

"Thanks for interrupting, dork," he said.

"I wanted to watch too."

"Well, you should invite your own friends over to watch it," Ethan said, grabbing the remote and flipping the television to the home screen, where all the various streaming apps waited for us.

"You two were just hanging out," I said. "You'll see each other tomorrow. Besides, you're always up each other's asses anyway."

I earned a firm pillow right to the face for that one.

"God, you're a pain in the ass," Ethan said.

"I'm gonna tell Mom you cussed!"

"Shut up." He loaded up YouTube and picked a video from this Japanese American couple who mostly vlogged about their cats and how they decorated their apartment.

The apartment stuff was boring to me, but at least the cats were funny. They had one that kept climbing into the garbage cans, so there was an entire video of them trying to figure out how to keep him out.

The weird part was, I wished Marcus were still here. But I didn't scrutinize that too much. I started thinking about what Ethan had said, about having my own friends. But Joel and

Vanessa were together now, and it felt like they were more interested in being around each other than they were with me. I didn't like how it made me feel, so maybe if I got a boyfriend it would all even out?

"Hey, Ethan?" I leaned down on the couch, putting the pillow next to Ethan's leg before I lay down.

"What's up?"

"How do you get someone to like you?"

Ethan looked at me. "What do you mean?"

"You've got a girlfriend, so you know how that works, right?"

"Pfft." Ethan chuckled. "Yeah, right."

"But you've got someone you like. How'd you do that?"

"I don't know." Ethan looked at me and waited a beat before answering. "I just asked her if she wanted to go out."

"It was that easy?"

"I mean . . . not really." Ethan rubbed the back of his neck, suddenly seeming so unsure of himself. "We were friends for a while before that."

"Really?"

"Yeah, she, um . . . we hung out in middle school, then her parents moved her across town so she had to go to West Lenoir."

"That sucks."

"Yeah." Ethan finally met my eyes again. "Do you have a crush?"

"No . . . not really," I said quickly. There was no way he

could see how my mind had flashed to Marcus and then quickly pulled the image down.

"Well, you usually need one of those before you fall in love."

"I don't have anyone. I wish I did—it'd make things easier."

"What do you mean?"

"I don't know. I feel lonely sometimes."

"Like how?"

"Like when Joel and Vee started to date each other, and suddenly we went from hanging out every single weekend to them wanting to be alone."

"Couples usually want alone time, Lee."

"I know, but they were my friends, and I don't have anyone else. It just sucks that they want to hang out without me. It feels like they're ghosting me or something."

"Why don't you tell them that?"

"'Cause it wouldn't make sense," I said.

"Well, you don't make much sense now."

Of course he wouldn't understand. I wasn't even sure if *I* understood.

"Tell me," Ethan said.

"It's weird."

"Try me. I know a thing or two."

"So, like . . . I don't know, when they don't invite me out, I feel alone and weird and it hurts. But when they *do* invite me out, or when we're at lunch, or in the library or whatever, they're with each other and I'm just sitting there."

"Ouch, yeah, that sucks."

"I hate it."

"Well, they're in love. At least I'm guessing, so they're going to want to be around each other. But it does suck that they're totally dropping you. I hate couples like that."

"I miss them."

"Like I said before, maybe you should tell them that."

"Maybe."

"And who knows . . ." Ethan said, his voice turning suddenly solemn. "Maybe you guys weren't meant to be friends forever."

"I don't like that."

"I don't either, Lee, but it happens. If you don't drift apart now, it'll probably happen after you graduate."

"Maybe." I'd heard people talking all the time about how high school relationships never lasted after you graduated, but I'd always thought that meant romantic relationships, not platonic ones. But maybe Ethan was right, as much as I didn't want to admit it. Maybe we just weren't meant to be friends anymore. Maybe I deserved better, and maybe they deserved each other.

Still, it didn't make the sting go away. I hated the idea of not having Joel and Vanessa in my life anymore.

"Why is stuff so complicated?" I asked him.

Ethan laughed. "Oh, you have no idea. Get ready for things to get *way* more complicated."

"Please." I sat up. "You're not even that much older than me!"

"I'm old enough," he told me. "Now respect your elders." Ethen put his hand over my face and shoved me back down onto the couch.

"Hey!"

Ethan chuckled.

"Don't do that!" I said.

"Keep your voice down!"

"Whatever." I leaned against the opposite end of the couch, the arm digging into the small of my back. We settled into the comfortable silence of watching the television, where YouTube had shifted to cooking videos. Eventually we got tired and switched over to Hulu and turned on *Bob's Burgers*; old episodes that we'd seen three or four times by now started to play. I pulled my knees close to my chest. "Hey, Ethan?"

"Hmmm?" He hummed without taking his focus away from the TV.

"Are you in love with her?" I asked him.

"What?"

"The girl." I motioned to his phone. "Are you in love with her?"

"Yeah, I am." Ethan smiled. "I think I could spend the rest of my life with them."

"That's good," I said. "Will we ever get to meet her?"

"You will." Ethan turned back to the television, and I took that as a sign that the conversation was over, even though I had a thousand more questions.

I tried to make myself comfortable, grabbing another pillow to rest my head on. I don't know at what point I fell asleep, but it was early when I woke up the next morning, so early that the sky was still painted orange and blue and purple with the rising sun. The television was off, and the only sound I could hear were the birds chirping just outside the window.

There was a blanket draped over me too.

One that I didn't remember taking, but I was glad to have it because my feet were feeling cold.

I stretched my legs out, feeling the empty space at the other end of the couch where Ethan had been last night, but I didn't feel him. I rolled over, turning the decorative couch pillow over to the side that wasn't so scratchy, and I quickly began to fall asleep again.

after

I was curious.

That was all.

I had another twenty minutes before Vanessa would be picking me up for school. Mom had finally decided to go back to work, so now I'd be relying on Vanessa and Joel for rides.

As I prepared to march myself down the stairs, I stopped at Ethan's door again and went inside. The room was as it had been days ago—Ethan's bed unmade, the shelves on the walls holding his trophies. A small baseball helmet that had once held ice cream from our Atlanta vacation, his actual baseball helmet that he'd outgrown so now instead it sat on display.

I sat down on the edge of the bed, staring at myself in the mirror that hung above his dresser. We looked too alike, too much like our mother. The same sloped nose, ears that were a touch too big and stood out just enough to be noticeable.

When we were kids, Ethan used to call me Dumbo, but then I'd say his ears were just like mine and he didn't like that very much. It was only fun when he was teasing me and not the other way around.

I didn't know what I was looking for in his room now. I didn't even know that there was something that I was looking for. Perhaps I just felt like, in that moment, I wanted to be closer to him. I wanted to see where he'd spent some of his last moments, where he'd been before he'd decided to get dressed and go for a run.

I remembered him being so depressed that day. Mom and Dad always chalked it up to just being a regular teenager, but I didn't know if I believed that or not. I'd had fleeting moments of depression and sadness; whatever Ethan had been going through, it was worse. Like worse as in he hardly ate and rarely ever left his room worse.

Granted, Ethan was always sort of a grumpy guy. But I remembered those days leading up to the accident as being some of the worst.

That's why Mom had asked me to invite him to the mall with us.

I stood up, fluffed his pillows, pulled back the sheets, and made his bed. I found the shoes he'd been wearing, the ones that the coroner let us keep in exchange for the suit that he was buried in, and I placed them in his closet, in the spot where he normally kept them. I took some of the clothing that he'd left out, unwashed and unhung, and slipped it into the dirty-clothes hamper near his door.

I heard the honking first, then the buzzing in my pocket.

Vanessa was calling me.

"Hey, sorry," I apologized. "I'll be right out."

"Okay, hurry up." I could hear the newest BTS song playing loudly in the background. Good to know that she'd moved on from Weyes Blood's last album.

"Okay," I said, shutting the door to Ethan's room behind me. "I'll be down in five."

"Make it three, Cooper—we're burnin' daylight here!" Vanessa said, deepening her already-prominent Southern accent.

"I'm a-comin'!" I told her with the same tone. I raced down the stairs, grabbing a banana from the fruit bowl before I walked out the back door, locking it behind me.

"There's a video I want to show the both of you" was the first thing Joel said to us when we walked up to our usual table in the cafeteria.

"Why do I feel like I'm going to regret letting you show this to me?" Vanessa asked.

"Because we will," I told her.

I picked my usual seat across from the two of them, right in front of Joel. Doctors would have probably described it as masochistic behavior, placing myself in front of my two best friends, who were so dangerously in love with each other they couldn't stand it. It wasn't healthy for me, not when I felt that ache of wanting someone like they wanted each other, I knew that.

But at the same time I didn't.

I just didn't seem to comprehend it at all.

"Here." Joel laid his phone out so both Vanessa and I could see, though I had to watch most of it upside down. It was a ludicrous and surreal comedy skit from a show I didn't recognize where this woman was absolutely furious over no one in her office laughing at her joke about Santa bringing a printer early. Joel was losing it five seconds in, shoving his face into his arms and quietly pounding his fist on the table.

Vanessa and I both watched as it devolved into absolute absurdity, with crying and shouting.

"What is this?" she asked.

"It's a show on Netflix. I found it last night and needed you both to see it."

"Hilarious," I said, pulling out my own phone to check on absolutely nothing. "I'd be down to watch it."

"Yeah, let's do it Friday, if you're both free." Joel took his phone back. "Here's another one—this is my actual favorite."

"I can't do Friday, babe, you know that."

"What? Why?" Joel asked in his most pretend whiny voice.

"I told you, that's the night my mom's boss is doing this dinner party thing for the company, and Dad roped me into going," Vanessa said, forlorn. "But you two should just do it without me. You both basically have the same warped sense of humor."

"We do not," I protested, though I wasn't sure why.

"Remember that video of that girl, and every time she opened her mouth it was just digital beep-boop sounds? You both lost your shit for a week after that. And when Lee was obsessed with those TikTok cringe compilations."

"Those were hilarious. You can't argue that," I told her.

"I most certainly can."

"What do you think about that?" Joel asked me, that mischievous smile on his face.

"Think about what?" I asked.

"You can come over, we'll cook some dinner or maybe go through a drive-thru, hang out just the two of us."

"Sure, that sounds like fun."

"And we'll hang out Saturday night?" Joel grabbed Vanessa's hand, snuggling up against her, his head resting in the crook of her neck.

"Yeah, babe, of course." Vanessa pulled him closer, kissing his forehead.

"Are you sure you don't want me to just go to that dinner with you?" Joel asked.

I didn't want to show the hurt I felt at this question. We'd *just* made the plans seconds ago, and now Joel was already threatening to cancel them while I sat right in front of him.

"No, it'll be fine. I don't want you to have to suffer," Vanessa told Joel.

"You're so cute." Joel wrapped his arms around her.

And I just had to sit there and watch.

I didn't want them to break up; I didn't want either of them to lose each other, or lose me. But I wished that I could've gone back in time, gotten them to stop falling in love with each other so fast. Who knows, maybe that wouldn't work. Perhaps they were always destined to be together, and maybe we were destined to drift apart because of this. I couldn't tell the future, and I didn't know which reality would be worse. If they broke up, I'd be forced to pick between them. Or, if they stayed together, then I didn't know how much longer I could be their friend, content to sit on the sidelines of their relationship while they both remained in an ignorant bliss as to how I really felt.

I couldn't wish for this to be different. Couldn't cast a spell or hope a fairy godmother would help me find the answer. The same way that I couldn't wish Ethan back to life.

The world didn't work that way, even if I wanted it to.

"You want to ride home with me?" Vanessa asked me fifth period. "I really want to show you this song."

"Um . . ." I looked up from the doodle I'd been doing in the corner of my biology study guide.

"Come on, when's the last time we worked together on something? Just you and me?" Vanessa leaned her head down on the desk, staring up at me. "You've totally been ghosting me."

Her question was funny to me because I could've asked her the same thing, guilt-tripped her with all the weekends I'd spent alone.

"I have not," I told her.

"Have too," she pouted.

"Have not." I went back to my doodle, which I was very invested in.

"Cute cats," she said.

"Thanks."

"For real, it's been too long since it was just us. You and Joel are gonna have your guys' night out—"

I shot her a look.

"Okay, your guy and enby night in, where you watch awful Netflix movies and braid each other's hair."

"Better," I said.

"I really want to show you this song, and I got the stems from the last CRJ single."

I looked up at her quickly. "No way."

Vanessa just grinned, as if I'd handed her a gold medal or something.

"How did you—"

"I've got my sources," she said, attempting to project an air of mystery.

"So, Reddit?"

"I know a guy . . ." Vanessa told me.

"So, Reddit," I repeated.

"The r/stems forum has a lot of gems if you dig through the awful shit."

"I imagine," I told her. "Sure, let's do it."

She wanted to hang out one-on-one, that was what I wanted—so why wouldn't I take Vanessa up on her offer?

"Thank God. I thought I was going to have to kidnap you."

I snorted. "You couldn't do that."

"I could kidnap you in my sleep."

"My, my, talks of kidnapping?" I heard Mr. Johnson, our Algebra III teacher, before I saw him. The man was like a ghost, always appearing out of nowhere when you least expected him to. "I sure hope Liam will have plenty of time to study while he's all tied up."

"I'll try to make the time, Mr. Johnson," I told him.

"Good." He patted me on the shoulder, and Vanessa stared up at him. "Until then, make sure you're still studying. We can't let kidnappings get in the way of a good education."

"Yes, Mr. Johnson," I said, and that was enough for him because he moved on.

When he was back at his desk, looking at a set of papers, Vanessa just barely turned back to face me. Our eyes met, and we laughed with each other.

After the final bell rang, I waited for Vanessa.

And waited.

And waited.

I leaned against her car in the student parking lot, watching my classmates who didn't have large bouts of anxiety when it came to even the mention of being behind a wheel.

I'd tried a year before to learn how to drive. Dad had taken me to the parking lot of the county fair, a place that, ten months out of the year, was a simple dirt field with the barest hints of driving paths. He'd tried and tried and tried to teach me, but no matter how many times I got behind the wheel, my nerves always got the best of me. Things only got worse when Ethan talked to me about other drivers and wrecks. Then I'd look up statistics about accidents and driving-related deaths.

(I only realized the irony of that later.)

I pulled out my phone and texted Vanessa.

ME: I'm by your car.

ME: Still hanging out right???

ME: hurry please, I'm sweating!!!!!!!

There was no answer.

I sighed, watching as the parking lot emptied. I pulled at my shirt, which was feeling tight against my chest as the sun hung high in the sky. It was a hot day for April, and it was only worse because I'd been leaning against a hot metal car.

I glanced across the yard at the wood- and auto-shop classes, situated inside old-style garages where the large doors had been left open so that the students inside might catch a breeze. To my surprise, I saw Marcus walking across the yard, his shoulders hunched as he moved closer to the baseball field.

What is he doing? I thought.

I looked around, as if anyone cared what I was doing or where I was going, and then I started to follow Marcus. He was heading right where I'd expected him to go. I watched as he moved closer to the baseball field, leaping over the fence before he strolled into the dugout. I walked a little farther down to the gate, unlatching it. I felt nervous at the idea of being caught.

I wanted to find Marcus, though. I wanted to talk to him again.

I walked into the dugout.

"Marcus?"

"Hmm?" He turned to me, not seeming shocked in the slightest that I was here. "Liam."

"Hey," I said. "I saw you and wanted to see where you were going. I wanted to make sure you were okay, after the other day."

"Oh . . . um, yeah." Marcus stared at the ground, kicking up the dust that covered the concrete.

"So . . ." I stared at him. "Are you?"

"What?"

"Okay?"

"I mean . . . it's whatever."

"You don't have to lie," I told him. "Least of all to me."

"I don't want to talk about this, Lee."

"If you can't talk about it with me, then who can you talk to about it? Who can *I* talk to about it?"

"A therapist?"

I supposed he had a point.

"Look—you weren't at the funeral."

"You noticed."

"Kind of hard not to," I said. "You were his best friend."

"Yeah." Marcus leaned down, taking a seat on the uncomfortable bench.

"Why weren't you there?" I asked flatly.

"You just wouldn't understand."

"You could try explaining it."

"And you could try leaving me the fuck alone," he said, his voice raised, glare focused directly on me.

"You were his best friend and you weren't there," I repeated. I couldn't leave without an explanation. Though I wasn't sure if

I actually wanted one, or if I just wanted something that would make Marcus a good guy again.

He stood up. "I didn't come here to have you breathing down my fucking neck."

"I think you owe me an answer," I told him.

"And *I* think that I don't owe you shit." Marcus stepped toward me, and for the first time since I'd known him, I was scared of him. "You don't know what it's been like, Liam. You may think you do, but you don't." I saw the tears welling, the way his hands shook with anger.

"I was his brother."

"Yeah, well, none of that matters anymore anyway." Marcus looked so pained, his face contorted in discomfort. And then I finally saw the scared boy who stood in front of me.

"He would've wanted you there," I said. "We all wanted you there."

"Get out," he said.

I stood there, waiting for him to do something.

Anything.

"I said *get the fuck out!*"

I didn't wait another second—I simply obeyed. I walked backward out of the dugout, not taking my eyes off Marcus until I was a safe distance away. Then I bolted back to the parking lot. Every time I blinked, I could still see the way Marcus's face had twisted through my memory, the scowl, the tears, the way he shook with anger and pain.

In the moment I'd just wanted answers. Now, after, I realized I'd probably wound up hurting him more.

Ethan had been Marcus's best friend.

He'd lost someone too.

And Marcus was right—they talked much more than Ethan and I ever talked. Marcus truly knew him better, knew him more.

Maybe he'd known that there was no way he'd survive seeing his best friend buried.

Maybe I should've felt the same way.

I felt that guilty twist in my stomach as I slowed my pace, looking back at the dugout, wondering if I should go apologize to him. But then my phone began to vibrate.

Vanessa.

"Hey," she said when I answered the call.

"Hey, where are you?" I asked, not thinking.

"I'm in my car. Where are you?" she asked.

"Sorry, I had to go get something I forgot," I told her.

"Hmph. And *I'm* the one with a bunch of missed texts asking me where I am."

"Well, I waited for a while."

"Just get over here, Cooper," she said.

In my head, I knew it was a joke. She hadn't meant it

seriously, but it still stung that she was being that condescending with me.

"There you are," Vanessa said as I climbed into the passenger seat. "What'd you forget?"

"My math book," I lied.

"Of course." Vanessa laughed, and I was getting more irritated with every passing second.

"Well, you were taking forever," I said. "So I thought I had time."

"Yeah, well, I wanted to spend a little time with Joel and I kind of forgot."

Of course.

I didn't reply. I just let her think she'd won some nonexistent argument against me as she put the car into drive and pulled out of her spot.

We bobbed our heads to FKA twigs on the ride to her house, and I tried hard not to think about how I'd been forgotten.

Again.

I was getting sick of being two people's second best.

Vanessa had a whole lot of impressive equipment at her house. The PC that her mom had helped her build, her guitars, her recording equipment, her speakers. I was so envious of her setup that sometimes it actually made me feel like less of a musician than her.

Which was silly, of course.

"Okay, so here's what I wanted to show you," Vanessa said, throwing her backpack on her bed and going right for her desk chair. I grabbed a chair from the dining room across the hall and planted it next to hers.

Vanessa pulled up the audio file, handed me her earphones, and I sat back and listened to the quiet beat that she'd produced. There were light vocals, with filters over them to make her sound otherworldly. These wind chimes came in, and then the strained sound of her guitar. It reminded me of FKA, or maybe Janelle Monáe mixed with some Billie Eilish. It was an incredibly good song, but I knew that it would be before I even slid on the headphones. It flooded me with jealousy, and I sat there wishing that I could've come up with something even half as good as this song sounded, or that I had access to an expensive program like Ableton too.

"It's amazing," I told her, my voice noticeably flat, as if I were lying.

I wasn't, but I was still bitter about everything that'd happened today, and my mind was still focused on Marcus and what was going on there.

I needed to apologize to him.

"Really?" Vanessa stared at me carefully, as if she were expecting me to drop a house on her or something. "You don't hate it?"

"I'd tell you if I hated it."

Even if we held back about everything else, we were always honest about each other's music. We never gave each other feedback unless we honestly believed it would make the song better.

"I like how quiet the intro is." I handed her the headphones. "I think you need a heavier drop, something more dramatic. So it almost sounds like a choir song. That'll sell the emotion."

Vanessa looked at her screen and chewed on her thumb. "You're right."

"Here, can I—?"

"Yeah, do it." We switched seats, and I slipped the headphones back on, searching through her extensive library of sounds, testing out a few before I settled on something that I thought was appropriate for the song. Then I added a few samples, lowered the pitch so it would have the *boom!* we were looking for.

"And . . ." I cleaned some details. "There, I think that's something."

"I'll switch to the speakers. They have a better bass."

I waited until Vanessa gave me the go-ahead, then hit play. I made sure to back up her vocals, overlay them so that there was this doubling effect in some areas. I'd really wanted to experiment with the haunting sound of Vanessa's voice. I'd added a snare as well, and a few sharper drum kicks.

Vanessa bobbed her head. "Holy shit."

"You like it?" I scrolled through the song, watching the

bottom of the screen as it played. I could already hear a few things I wanted to change. It wasn't as crisp as I wanted it to be. But overall I still enjoyed it. I liked most of the songs that I made, and I could never tell if that was a good or a bad thing. It had to be good, right?

"Do you want to post it?" I asked Vanessa, going right to Google Chrome and typing in SoundCloud so her URL would come up.

"Maybe." She watched the screen. "Do you think it's worth it?"

I smiled at her. "Yeah, do it."

Vanessa grinned back.

I understood the hesitation; I always struggled when it came to posting something online. That feeling of questioning whether or not it was actually finished, or if I was just tired of working on it.

I pulled up the file on the upload page and dragged it right in.

"I've got the art to go along with it on my desktop."

I flipped back to the desktop and added the album art. "Do you have the YouTube version ready to go?" I asked as I hit the upload button.

"Yeah." Vanessa took the mouse and clicked her way to her YouTube page, where she started the upload process. I couldn't help but eye the 10,794 subscribers she boasted, knowing that I wanted that too.

I just needed to work as hard as Vanessa did.

"What else have you been hiding up here?" I took the mouse back, going to her SoundCloud profile again and clicking through her drafts. Songs that she'd either forgotten or had second thoughts about.

One new song caught my eye because of its title.

"Binh."

Joel's Vietnamese name.

"What's this?" I hovered the mouse over it, knowing that what I was about to hear would only serve to hurt me, not help me.

Vanessa blushed. "Oh—that's a song for Joel."

"A love song?" I prodded.

"Maybe." Vanessa covered her face. "Shut up."

"What? I'm just curious."

"You're making fun of me," she said.

"Yeah, and. You make fun of me all the time."

"I hate you."

"Hate you too." I looked at her, then the screen, then back to her. "Why didn't you release it?"

"Because . . ."

"Because?"

"Because I wrote it before we started dating. And I thought about posting it because you know he doesn't pay attention to this account, like even a little bit. So I thought it'd be safe, but then . . ."

"Then?"

"He asked me out, and I was worried that posting the song would jinx it or something, I don't know." Vanessa stopped. "That sounds stupid."

"Yeah," I teased, "it does."

"Shut up!" She shoved me, nearly pushing me out of the chair.

"No, it's adorable," I said through gritted teeth. "And I get it."

"You've never written a love song."

"No, I haven't."

Lie.

"Why not?"

"Because I've never had anyone to write one about."

"You've never been in love with anyone, Liam? Not once?"

"Nope, not even once. Not romantically, at least."

"That's sad."

I thought about her words for a moment, letting them sink in.

"You're telling me," I said, wanting this conversation to end. I focused back on the screen. "Can I hear it?"

"You want to hear my Joel song?"

I nodded, fully aware that I was cursing myself.

She turned off the speakers and gave me back the headphones. When they were comfortable, I pressed play. The guitar came first, and then her vocals.

There was nothing else to the song.

No drums, no snares, no synths, no effects or computer trickery except the mastering.

It was simply a girl and her guitar. Singing about shaved heads and hot summers, about a boy binding his chest and transforming, walking along the railroad tracks, and about loving someone with two names and two languages, two homes and two families. Dreaming and kissing and loving and holding.

I wanted to scream.

The song was too beautiful.

"Well . . ." Vanessa prodded, and that was when I realized I'd just been staring at the computer screen, my legs tucked up to my chest, watching as the computer waited for me to select another song.

"I love it," I said, slipping off the headphones.

"Really? You didn't think it was too cheesy or whatever?"

"No." I stared at her, hoping that my eyes wouldn't betray me. "It sounds perfect."

"I still don't know what I'll do with it."

"You could play it for him."

"I . . . I don't know." Vanessa looked away, as if to save herself the embarrassment. "It's whatever. I'll probably never do anything with it."

I wasn't going to argue with her. If she never showed Joel the song, maybe he wouldn't fall deeper in love with her.

tuesday, april 16, 2019

I was foolish in my belief that grief was a straightforward thing. I thought the first wave would hit, and gradually the feelings of sadness and desperation would slip away until I found myself normal again. But I was so very wrong.

Because grief is a complicated, ugly, messy thing.

And it makes you do complicated, ugly, messy things.

About three weeks after Ethan died, things started to get worse.

I'd gotten home and gone straight to my room, leaving my homework forgotten in my backpack as I attempted to crack another song. Try as I might, though, I couldn't figure it out.

Frustrated, I planned on walking down to the kitchen to check in on Mom and Dad, see what they were up to. Instead I found them inside Ethan's room, his door barely cracked, a little line of light coming from the window reflecting on the floor in the hallway.

"Do we save these?" I heard Dad ask.

"Save anything that's Liam's size. We'll see if they want to wear it. If not, we'll take another trip to Goodwill," Mom answered.

I opened the already cracked door slowly, taking in the cardboard boxes and plastic tubs that were decorating the room in place of everything that Ethan had.

"What's going on?" I asked, already knowing the answer.

They were packing up his things.

"Oh, hi, honey," Mom said, eyeing the shirt in her hands. She looked tired; they both did. Even from here I could see the skin around their eyes rimmed red.

"Hey," I said. Then I repeated my question. "What's going on?"

Mom looked around at the room, a forlorn expression on her face. "We're packing up a few of his clothes."

I didn't think she could bring herself to say his name just yet, to talk about her son as if he wasn't her son anymore.

"Why?" I asked, looking at the piles and bags of clothes in front of them.

They were getting rid of him, these pieces of him. Tossed into a trash bag.

"Well . . . we thought that the clothes could go to people in need," Dad said. "And we can't just let his things sit here."

"It hasn't even been a month," I told them.

"Liam, we get it. We understand. But . . ." Mom was already struggling to string together her words. "We thought it would be best if we started the process. Help us get past things."

"You want to *get past* your son's death?" I asked, knowing that my words were as sharp as a blade. "You're getting rid of him."

Mom and Dad were cleaning the room of Ethan. They were packing up their son, his clothing. And what would come next? The books? The posters? The games? The bed? Would this room turn into a guest room? Would every inch of Ethan's life in this house be packed away under the guise of "moving on"?

"That's not fair, Liam," Dad said.

"What's not fair is that you're packing up his things," I told them, looking around the room. "You can't just get rid of him like that."

"That's not what we're doing," Mom said.

"Then what are you doing?"

"We're trying to get better," Dad said.

"Shouldn't this be about him, not you?" I mumbled, though I knew that they could hear me. I think in some warped way, I wanted them to.

"*Liam.*" Mom said my name forcefully, staring me down from her place across the room. "Apologize to your father right now."

"Sorry," I grumbled.

I could tell that this wasn't enough for her, but it wasn't an issue that either of them wanted to press.

Dad didn't say anything; he just went back to the closet. "I want you to look through these later," he told me. "See if there's anything you want to keep."

"What will you do with the stuff I don't want?" I asked.

"Goodwill seems like the best place for it all," Mom said.

"So they'll go to random strangers?"

"Well, if you don't want the clothes, where's the best place for them, Liam?" Mom asked. It was clear from her tone that she was getting sick of me. "At least this way people can use them, or else they'll just sit in the attic and be eaten by moths."

I kept pressing, though.

"I'll keep all of it, then."

"Okay, well, now you're just being obtuse on purpose," Dad said.

"No, I'm not."

"Liam." Mom dropped her grip on the bag in her hands. "I can't deal with this right now."

"Good—maybe you'll leave Ethan's stuff alone, then."

"Liam, you need to be quiet." Dad's voice cut through the room. "Go to your room right now."

I froze because Dad never really talked like this. Between him and Mom, he'd always been the pushover, always the one I'd go to if I was in trouble because I knew that he'd go easy on me.

"This isn't fair," I said.

"I agree," Mom said. "Nothing about this is fair. But we have to do this."

"What else are we supposed to do?" Dad asked. "Do you have the answer? It'd be great if you did because then maybe you could tell us."

"I—"

Dad held up his hand. "We're doing what we think is right, Lee. Maybe it won't be the right move, maybe it'll make things worse for us. But there's no way for us to know that."

I met Mom's gaze behind him, and there were tears already forming in her eyes. She wasn't crying, but they were wet; it was obvious that I'd upset her.

Dad's voice suddenly went quiet, as if he was afraid. I noticed the trembling in his hands. "We're doing our best. For us and for you. That's all we can do."

I didn't want to hear what else they had to say to me. I rushed out of the room. I barely had time to get back to my room and grab my worn yellow Vans. The ones that slipped onto my feet easily, that I never really wore anywhere because they were so dirty from mud and rain that I didn't want to be seen in them.

But they were comfortable.

I put them on and bolted down the stairs to the front door.

"Liam!" Mom shouted.

"Liam, we need to have a talk," Dad followed up.

"No!" I yelled back, pushing my way out the front door. I briefly entertained stealing a car from my parents, maybe Ethan's. I'd drive somewhere private, somewhere no one could find me. But I didn't even know how to drive yet, and all the keys were inside.

So, without a car, and in a town that didn't have ride sharing, I started to walk toward the street.

I walked.

Ethan ran.

I stayed near the side of the road, walking slowly on the dirt and through the knee-high weeds. It was filthy. There were broken amber bottles, plastic wrappers from snack cakes and chip bags, grocery bags left to drown in brown water.

I ignored the spot where Ethan had breathed his last breaths, still decorated by that orange X. And there was the cross, more crooked now. The flowers that looked alive when they were placed around it were now dried and dead, slowly being reclaimed by the Earth.

I didn't know where I was walking.

There was a small store at the end of our road. A place called Vance's Country Store that didn't seem similar to anything else I'd ever known. Mom used to stop by here every morning when she dropped us off at school, and we'd get biscuits to eat on the ride. The older we got, though, the more infrequent that became. At some point it closed, then opened back up again. As far as I could tell, there was nothing different about it at all, except that they no longer stocked gas in the pumps.

I'd walk there, then keep walking.

Joel's house was a ten-minute drive, which in my head added up to maybe thirty minutes of walking. Whatever happened, I knew that I'd be in trouble when I got back home.

I'd known that cleaning Ethan's room would be a thing that would happen. But still, it hurt me.

Maybe I'd wanted to make a scene. Maybe I'd wanted to hurt my parents, in some fucked-up way of getting back at them for not being able to stop something that was beyond their control. Maybe I felt I was their second-best option out of their two children. They'd lost the golden child, the all-American boy who would take care of them with his baseball career.

All they had left was me.

I walked until I met the chalky white parking lot of Vance's Country Store. The only proper spot of pavement was in front of the door. The rest of the yard was a white rock that kicked up far too much dust when a tire so much as crawled across the surface.

"Liam!"

I turned quickly in the direction of my father's voice. He pulled his car into the lot, the passenger-side window rolled down so I was certain there would be a microscopic layer of white dust on the inside of his car until he cleaned it next time.

"Get in the car."

I didn't argue with him. I didn't fight. Because I didn't have anywhere else to go. There were options, of course, but at the end of the day, as the sun dipped below the surface to pull the moon into place, I'd have to return home.

I climbed into the car, breathing in the dust. Dad pulled out of the lot and drove me back home. Back past where the ambulances had been parked, past where the news vans and camera crews had stood to cover the death of a "beloved Lenoir County teen," past the orange X.

Dad didn't say anything to me.

Perhaps he didn't have anything at all that he wanted to convey. Maybe he was that furious with me.

I'd be angry too.

I was angry.

And I was sorry.

But I didn't say those words. I didn't say them to him or to Mom as we walked inside. Neither of them demanded that I did. I walked up to my room, closed the door behind me, and slipped my headphones on, drowning out the rest of the world.

Dad dropped me off at school the next morning. Which was as awkward as it sounds. He said the bare minimum to me, letting me know we needed to leave in the next few minutes. He didn't tell me goodbye. He didn't even look at me.

I didn't say anything back.

I was still pissed that they'd been so eager to get rid of Ethan's things.

Did I need to go in and steal the things I wanted to keep? Were they under threat of being thrown away and forgotten? What about Marcus? How would he feel about seeing his best friend packed away and donated so easily?

Marcus.

I was determined to find Marcus, to apologize for how I'd made him feel. But until I actually found him, I had to pretend that everything was totally normal, and that my life wasn't falling apart at the seams.

"You look exhausted," Joel said to me as I took a seat at our usual breakfast spot.

"Yeah, well . . ." was the most of an answer that I could conjure up. I really wasn't in the mood for talking, especially after a night of barely sleeping. I'd tossed and I'd turned, but my mind kept conjuring everything I'd said to my parents just hours before, the things they'd said back to me, how guilty it'd all made me feel. And then I thought about Marcus and what I was going to say to him.

I couldn't empty my mind enough to allow it to sleep.

Vanessa didn't say anything in response to my nonanswer. She just stared at me and then looked away. Joel didn't say anything either. They were both quiet, which made me feel like something was wrong. Vanessa bit off a piece of the Honey Bun that she'd bought from the vending machine in the student center, and Joel pulled out his phone and started scrolling through Instagram. They'd seemed to be having such a lively conversation before I'd gotten here.

So I guessed that meant I was the piece of this equation that fucked everything up.

"Well, don't talk my ear off," I said.

"Sorry." Vanessa covered her mouth to yawn. "Didn't get much sleep last night. I was up late."

"Aw, come here." Joel wrapped his arm around her, pulling her in close. "You need your eight hours to keep that brain fresh, babe."

"Oh, please." She rolled her eyes. "Like you have any room to talk. What time did you go to bed last night?"

"Irrelevant. My hormones keep me up at night."

She looked at him. "That doesn't make any sense, *and* you're avoiding the question."

"Because I don't want to admit that you're right," Joel said with a smile.

Vanessa shoved him away. "I hate you."

Joel wrapped her up again, throwing both his arms around her. "You love me!"

"Do not."

"Say it! Say you love me!" He threw on this cutesy high-pitched voice that was grating on my nerves so early in the morning.

"No," Vanessa protested, a smile on her face. "I hate you."

"You lie!" Joel cried out, burying his face in Vanessa's shoulders.

I was going to be sick.

"Say you love me," he said.

"No!"

"Say you love meee!"

Vanessa made eye contact with me, as if to say, *Can you believe this?* But we both knew how clingy Joel could be. How he wanted to drape his body over yours when he lay down on the couch, or how he always wanted to hold Vanessa's hand when we were out in public. Right now was the perfect example actually, the way he craved her touch in the middle of this cafeteria.

"I'm going to the bathroom," I told them, unable to watch this anymore. I grabbed my backpack and walked out of the cafeteria, not waiting for either of them to say anything to me.

I walked right past the bathrooms, not really sure where I was going. I had about twenty minutes before the bell for class rang, so I thought I could afford to go anywhere I wanted. I headed outside, desperate for the nice April breeze that was blowing through the air. I almost expected Vanessa or Joel to pop out of one of the doors, following me, asking me where I was going. But apparently I was too hopeful that they'd care.

Maybe Ethan had been right. Maybe we'd just outgrown one another. I stopped by the student board that was in the middle of the courtyard in the center of campus, the glass-encased bulletin board where students were allowed to post things like club flyers, advertisements for tutoring, all those kinds of things. The glass was supposed to keep the flyers from blowing away, but everyone knew that it was to keep students from being able to post advertisements for good times, or pictures calling someone a ho. It also discouraged the drawing of penises on everything, though, only minimally.

I looked over my options, maybe to see if there was an advertisement for any people who wanted to be friends.

How sad was that?

Looking for friends on a school bulletin board.

Maybe there was a club I could join, or a tutoring session I could teach. Not that I was smart enough to tutor anyone, but maybe that could be a fast way to meet someone.

Unfortunately, with the school year coming to a close in just a few weeks, all the deadlines to join clubs had passed. So the board was filled with advertisements for a bake sale, a student flea market next weekend in the parking lot, the school play that was going on at the end of April. And underneath all that, I could spy Ethan's name, some tribute to him.

No clubs, no friends, no lonely person reports.

Nothing.

Just bake sales and dead brothers.

Suddenly, I felt so lonely, having put all my stock into my only two friends. I'd never thought that they'd abandon me. I never pictured losing the two of them. How could they be comfortable with this? They had to feel me slipping away; they had to know that I was distancing myself.

Right?

I walked away from the board, hanging my head in shame as I walked closer to the student parking lot, then farther, to the baseball field.

To the dugout.

Maybe he's there today.

As I walked through the grass that was still wet and caused the clay-colored dirt to gather and stick to the bottoms of my Converse, I saw him sitting in the dugout.

He was hunched over, a book in his hands, which surprised me. And then I felt like an asshole for assuming Marcus wouldn't do something as simple as read.

Marcus didn't even turn to look at me as I sauntered in.

"Here to yell at me some more?" he asked, wetting his fingers before he turned a page.

"No," I said. "What are you reading?"

"Are you going to police what I read now?"

"You don't have to—" I stopped myself. I didn't need to fight with Marcus; I needed his help. "Marcus, I'm sorry."

These were the words that got him to finally look at me.

I went on. "I'm sorry for cornering you the other day and asking you all that invasive stuff and for being an asshole. I'm sorry, I really am."

"Well . . ." He folded down the corner of the page he'd been reading. "That's a start, I suppose."

"I really am sorry."

"Why do I get the feeling that you want something?"

"I don't. I promise. I understand why you weren't at the funeral—"

"Please stop talking about the goddamn funeral, Liam. *Please.*"

I opened my mouth again, but stopped short of saying the words *I'm sorry*. Instead I said, "Okay."

"You were a real asshole. I hope you know that." He looked at me out of the corner of his eye.

"Yeah, I know."

"Okay." He leaned back, setting his book to the side.

"Is that it?" I asked.

"Did you expect something else?"

I slid my backpack off my shoulders and set it on the bench so that I could sit down next to him.

"Is there a reason you weren't at the funeral?" I asked, because I couldn't help myself. "You only have to answer that if you want to. I just want to know why."

"You know, curiosity killed the cat," Marcus said, before he went back to his book.

"But satisfaction brought him back," I finished.

"What?"

"That's the other part of the saying. Everyone forgets that," I told him.

Marcus chuckled, shaking his head at me. "You're too smart for your own good, Liam. Always were."

"My parents are getting rid of Ethan's things."

That got Marcus's attention. "What?"

"They were going through his clothes, ready to donate them," I said. "We had a fight about it last night."

"Oh . . . well . . . that sucks."

Was that all Marcus had to add? I felt like there was something else. I watched as his body language changed, his foot started tapping uncomfortably, and his shoulders became a little more hunched over.

I ventured, "You don't want to go and talk any sense into them?"

Marcus looked back at me. "That's not my job. If they want to get rid of his things, then that's their choice."

"You know, I expected you out of everyone would care about this . . . but I guess I was wrong."

His attention went back to his book. "I guess you were."

In the distance, we could both hear the bell for first period.

"Sounds like you should go to class," Marcus said to me. "Unless you want to go to ISS."

I thought about staying with him, hiding here. I most certainly didn't want to see Vanessa during first period. But I knew that I wouldn't get anything out of Marcus if I stayed.

So I walked away, back toward school, and back toward my classes. I turned around exactly once, to check and see if Marcus was behind me. He wasn't. He was stuck back there, as I moved forward. And yet it still felt like we were both stuck in the same place.

sunday, march 24, 2019

before

H ey, Mom?" I poked my head into the kitchen.

Mom was on her laptop, and from my point of view, it seemed like she was just scrolling through Facebook.

Clearly I wasn't bothering her.

"What's up?" she asked without looking at me.

"Vanessa wants to go to Goldsboro, and Joel's going with her. Can I go?"

"On a school night?" Mom pulled back her sleeve to check the Apple Watch that Dad had given her for their last anniversary. "I don't know about that, Lee."

"What? Come on, it's thirty minutes, and Vanessa can't even stay out that long; her curfew's at nine."

"Where are you going to go?" She sighed.

I shrugged. "Dunno, I think Vanessa wants to go to Forever 21."

"Are you going to get dinner while you're out?"

"Maybe."

"Grab a twenty from my purse, just in case."

"Hell yeah!" I jumped, going for her purse where she'd put it on the kitchen counter, right where it always was.

"Language." She eyed me. "*And* you have to do something for me."

"Oh God." I threw my head back, already exhausted by what might be coming next. "I'll help Dad put out the new pine straw next week." Even if it did always leave my skin itchy and irritated, and pine straw could really hurt if it poked you.

"No, that's not it." Mom's eyes followed mine. "Bring me my purse."

I grabbed it and brought it over to her, but the twenty was right near the top of her bag, in a little pocket I could already see.

"I want you to invite your brother."

"What?" I looked down the hallway, at the stairs, as if he were there on the landing, looking down at us. "I'm not doing that."

"Lee—"

"He's a jerk, and he doesn't want to hang out with Vanessa and Joel anyway. He'll just ruin the whole thing."

"No, he won't." Mom sighed. "Your brother has been really depressed lately." She had so much worry in her eyes.

"He's got his own friends. He can call Marcus."

"I think that might be the problem," she told me. "I think they had a fight or something; I don't know. He won't tell me what's wrong when I ask him."

"Well, that's not my fault."

Mom gave me the kind of look that had me ready to run and hide.

"Your brother could use some cheering up. Just do this, for me?"

I looked at her, then back up at the stairs. I didn't want to bring Ethan along; he wouldn't even want to go—who wants to spend an evening with their younger sibling and their friends? He'd just sulk the entire time anyway. I didn't know what had happened after I'd helped him practice his pitching the other day. Marcus had rushed out of the house that afternoon, not long after he'd gotten there, and ever since, Ethan had been a depressed mess.

He hardly ate anything at dinner, and if he wasn't in school or at practice, he was in his room, the Bluetooth speaker on his bedside table playing the last Lorde album.

I'd never seen him act like this before. And the last thing I wanted him to do was to ruin a fun night out with Joel and

Vanessa. It'd already been weeks since I'd gotten the chance to hang out with them outside school.

I groaned. "Ugh, fine."

"Thank you." She gave me the twenty and patted me on the shoulder, giving me permission to leave.

I raced up the stairs, thinking about how I was going to avoid asking Ethan to go out with us.

I stopped in front of his door and felt the crumpled twenty in my hand. I knocked slowly, and he didn't say anything. Didn't tell me to come in or go away.

"Ethan?" I didn't poke my head in, for fear of having something thrown at me. "You up?"

He didn't answer, and for a moment I wondered if he was even home. But of course he was home; his car was in the driveway.

"What?" I heard his voice, sharp and distant at the same time.

"Hey."

"What do you want, Lee?"

"Nothing," I lied. "Just checking on you."

I opened the door. He was lying on his bed, his face turned away from me so that I couldn't see it.

"I'm fine," he said.

"No, you're not."

"What the fuck do you know?" he asked, his voice quieter this time.

"You know you can tell me what happened," I said. "I won't tell Mom and Dad."

"Like that time you swore you wouldn't tell them that it was me and Marcus who put firecrackers in that drainage pipe across the street?"

"I—" That happened when I was eight; there was no way he still held a grudge over that.

"Just leave me alone, Liam."

"I don't like to see you sad."

"I'm not sad. Just leave me alone."

"You've been in your room all weekend—"

I narrowly ducked away from a rectangular tissue box aimed at my head.

"I said leave me the fuck alone, Lee!"

I paused, staring at Ethan as he readjusted himself on his bed. The room was a complete mess, with clothes thrown everywhere. And it smelled too, more so than usual.

Ethan's room only had one window, and that faced the back of the house, so even when the blinds weren't drawn, the room stayed dark. Now, with the blinds closed, the darkness of the room seemed more eerie than anything else.

I picked up the tissue box and threw it back at him. "What the hell is wrong with you?"

Ethan flinched when it struck him.

"I was just trying to help, asshole."

"Leave me alone."

"You keep saying that—"

"Because that's what I want."

"Maybe if you just talked your shit out, you wouldn't feel like absolute shit." I gargled my words.

"You wouldn't understand." Ethan slumped back onto the bed, muffling himself in his pillows. "I just want to sleep."

"All you've been doing is sleeping." Then I whispered, "Asshole." And left Ethan to do whatever it was that he wanted to do. By the time I'd gotten back to my room, I could see out the window that Joel and Vanessa were both waiting for me.

I shut Ethan's door and grabbed my bag from my room before I went down the stairs, hoping in vain that Mom wouldn't notice that he wasn't with me.

"Where's your brother?" she asked.

I'd already had my hand on the doorknob, ready to race outside.

So close.

"He said no."

"He doesn't want to go?" Mom stared at me, worried.

"Nope." Ethan didn't want to leave the house—he'd told me as much himself. So that was that.

Mom sighed, rubbing her palm along her forehead as if she were sweating.

"Can I still go?"

"Huh?" She looked at me like she'd forgotten I was there. "Yeah, sure, honey. Go have fun with your friends."

"Thanks, Mom."

"Don't be out too late."

"I won't be!" I said, the door almost already shut.

I raced around to the front of the house and hopped into the back seat of Joel's car.

I didn't give Ethan another thought.

after

Things at home didn't get any easier as the days stretched on. Dad didn't want to talk to me, and I didn't want to talk to him. Any words that we exchanged were simple, necessary. Dad asked me if Joel or Vanessa could pick me up from school, or if I was okay with his dinner plans.

That was all he had to say.

Which was still more than what Mom had to say to me.

I hadn't seen them cleaning out Ethan's room any more than they already had. It was a task left half done, trash bags waiting on the floor, full of shirts, pants, sweaters, and jackets he'd never wear again. Mom and Dad had only gotten so far as getting two boxes to put his more fragile belongings in. And beside them was a pile of books stacked precariously, things he'd had to read for class.

I heard someone walking around in the kitchen underneath me, so I left the room before going through the boxes.

I'd been watching my phone ever since Vanessa had dropped me off from school, waiting to see when Joel was going to swing by to pick me up. He hadn't even mentioned our plans today, but I assumed that they were still on. He'd come and pick me up, take me to his house, and we'd stay up way too late watching that show that he wanted me to watch and playing *Zelda* or *Smash Bros.*

But the closer the clock inched to five, the more worried I became. It would've been fine if he'd told me that he was picking me up at six or whatever, but there was a sinking feeling in my gut that wouldn't go away.

Joel answered his phone after the third ring. "Hey, what's up?"

"Are you still coming by to pick me up?"

"Oh, um . . ." Joel paused. "Did we have something planned?"

"Yeah," I told him, unable to hide the surprise in my tone. "We were going to hang out at your house tonight. Vanessa has that dinner party and you wanted to show me that thing on Netflix."

"Fuck. Right. God." I could hear his movement on the other side of the line, the groaning, his hand hitting his face. "I totally spaced on that."

"It's cool," I told him, even though it was decidedly not cool that he'd just completely forgotten about me. "Can you still come get me?"

"Oh, um . . . I'm sorry, Lee. I told Vanessa that I'd go with her to the dinner."

"But she said that she didn't need you to be there."

"I know, but I thought that it'd be a good idea if I went—you know, as her boyfriend and all."

"Oh. Okay," I said, but in my head, I wanted to say so much more. It was bullshit, it was so unfair, how could he have done this to me?

"I'm really sorry, Liam."

"It's fine, I, um . . ." I could feel the tears coming. "It's cool."

I think Joel heard my crying too.

"What I— Liam . . ."

"I'll see you on Monday, I guess." I didn't wait for his response, I just hung up the phone and threw it against my bed. It bounced off the mattress, hitting the wall at an angle that left a crack in the corner of the screen, and a small but still notice-able chip in the paint on my wall.

"Fuck me," I whispered to myself as I stared down at it. "Fuck a fucking fuck." I wanted to throw it again, to watch it shatter. How could he forget about me? How could they both forget about me, especially now? Vanessa *knew* that Joel and I had plans—and she'd just let Joel abandon me . . . again.

I looked at my phone, at the new crack there, and at my screensaver, simple sky blue, my favorite color. I thought about getting my shoes on and walking outside, walking and walking until maybe I reached Joel's house and I could curse him out more, or maybe call Vanessa and ask her why they both seemed so dedicated to leaving me behind.

But I didn't do any of those things.

Instead I called Marcus.

I hit dial, and his name appeared along the top of the screen. It rang and it rang. And for a moment I wondered if maybe he'd never put my contact information in his phone. Why would he? Was I just a random number that was blinking on his screen? Was he just like me, ignoring the random numbers that he hadn't saved himself under the belief that they were spam calls there to tell you about some new mortgage rate or an overdue credit card bill with a bank that you most certainly weren't a member of?

He picked up after the fourth ring.

"Hello?" His voice sounded rougher over the phone, deeper. "Liam?"

"Marcus?"

"Liam."

"Hey."

"What are you—why are you calling me?"

"Um . . . because I need someone to talk to."

"What do you mean?"

"Something happened—it's a long story."

"So your first instinct was to call me?"

"No, this was my fourth or fifth instinct."

"Ah, nice to know I'm so high up."

"So . . . what are you doing?"

"Well, I was taking a nap." He groaned as if he were sitting up. "I was going to go hang out with some friends later on tonight."

"Oh . . . that's nice."

"Liam."

"Huh?"

"Why did you call me?"

"Because my best friends are selfish and they've been ignoring me, and Joel just completely forgot that we'd already made plans for tonight so instead he's going out with Vanessa and I'm honestly just sick of the bullshit when it comes to those two and they've been ignoring me for a long time anyway, but I really thought they'd at least be here for me now, so I'm wondering if this is actually going to be a good thing and I—"

"Liam."

I stopped myself. I'd said all that with a single breath, and now my chest hurt a little bit. "Yeah?"

"You were talking a lot."

"Sorry. Um . . . how are *you* doing?"

"I'm okay, I guess." Marcus sighed, sounding tired more

than anything. "I'm supposed to be studying, but a nap sounded nicer."

"Oh, I'll let you sleep, then."

"Nah, it's okay. I probably should be up."

"But how are you going to study when you're on the phone with me?"

"Touché." Marcus let out this low laugh. "Liam . . ."

"Yeah?"

"Why did you call me?"

"I told you." I swallowed. "It's a long story."

"I've got time. We have a whole weekend for you to tell me."

"You don't want to hear about my problems."

"You're right—I don't."

I braced for the sting of his next words.

"But I'm going to anyway," he finished.

"Why?"

"You don't need to know why."

"Mysterious."

"I try."

"It's my friends," I said. "And my parents, and school, and everything with Ethan . . . it's, well—it's everything. It just hurts. It feels like I'm getting left behind. It just . . . I'm tired of feeling so alone."

"I know the feeling." And he sounded genuine. He didn't sound like he was lying to spare my feelings, or conjuring up emotions out of thin air just to make me seem like I wasn't spiraling out of control. "What happened with your friends?"

I talked for about ten minutes about Joel and Vanessa.

"And I get that they're in love or whatever," I said toward the end. "But. I feel like you can still have friends when you're in love. Right? I'm not an idiot in thinking that?"

"No, I wouldn't call you an idiot for that," Marcus said. "I've known lots of people who totally drop their friends for their boyfriends or girlfriends or whatever. It's never fun. And as much as I hate to say this, I find it only gets better when they're broken up."

"I don't want them to break up," I told him. "Then the three of us will never be friends again."

"Well, then, better get started on that time machine."

"If I had a time machine, that wouldn't be my priority."

"Right."

"Sorry."

"No, it's okay. Maybe your friends can break up amicably or whatever."

"Do you actually believe people can do that?"

"Honestly?"

"Yeah."

"No, I don't."

"Why not?"

"Why can't people be friends after they break up? Because

things get too intimate. If you date for long enough, you get to know the ins and outs of a person; you know them in a deeply personal way that you rarely can as a friend. And I just think that you can't go back."

"Wow . . . I didn't expect that answer from you."

"Yeah, well . . . I have experience."

"Yeah, you've probably dated, what, dozens of girls? A new girl every week, right?"

And he just let out this low, awkward laugh. "Yeah . . . no."

"Oh, come on, I've heard the rumors about you, Marcus. I heard in middle school that you were the first eighth grader to lose his virginity."

"And you actually believed that?"

"Um . . . yeah."

"Wow, okay. That was a total lie. I made it up so that Jackson Matthews would stop making fun of me."

"Oh . . ."

"And I don't have a girlfriend every week. Have you ever seen me with a girl?"

Suddenly, I was feeling very guilty for ever even believing these things about Marcus. "No . . . I guess not."

"I mean, if you had seen me with a girl, it'd be pretty weird."

"Why?"

"I'm gay, Liam."

"Wait, what?" I sputtered out, unable to stop myself. I

clamped my hand over my mouth, as if that'd do anything at all. "Wait—"

Suddenly, everything I knew about Marcus felt challenged. But was it really? I knew gay people. Vanessa and Joel both identified as bisexual, and Joel was open about being trans. There were also a few openly queer kids at East Lenoir as well, and a GSA even if there never seemed to be enough kids in the club to warrant having it. It also didn't change a thing about Marcus; he was gay before I knew this about him. But still, you can't help but rethink things when you find out something like this. It makes you see people in a different light, even if it shouldn't.

"Does that surprise you?"

"A little. I mean—I didn't know."

"Were you supposed to?"

I thought for a moment. "Guess not."

"It's not like it's a secret. I mean, I'm not out to everyone, just a few of my friends at school. I was out to Ethan, and now you, I guess. I just kind of thought it was one of those open secrets."

"I had no idea."

"Well, now you do."

"I'm gay," I said. "Too, I mean. Or queer or whatever, I don't really know yet."

"Huh."

"'Huh'? What do you mean, 'huh'?"

"I mean, I always got that vibe from you."

"What is that supposed to mean?"

"You don't think I noticed the way you stare at the guys on the baseball team?"

"I, um . . ."

"Nah, you're good. Those baseball pants do make our butts look nice."

"Oh." I said, my mouth suddenly dry. "Yeah, they do. Did Ethan ever tell you that I'm nonbinary?"

"No," Marcus said. "Should he have?"

Well, I hadn't wanted Ethan to tell anyone at school, but there was always that worry in the back of my head that Ethan would've shared that information with Marcus no matter what. Maybe I'd assumed the worst of Ethan.

"No."

"Everything okay, Liam?"

"Yeah, it's just . . . I don't know, you're the first person I've been able to talk to about this."

"Really?"

"Yeah, I mean, some of my friends are queer," I told him, not wanting to out Joel and Vanessa, though the two of them being my only actual friends probably made it more obvious than it should've been. "But we've never talked about it a ton, ya know. And Ethan and my parents, they told me they understood, but sometimes it's like they just don't get it."

"I know the feeling. Sometimes my dad asks if I'm sure I'm not interested in girls."

"Ouch—that sucks."

"Yeah, but what can you do? It's better than I ever expected in a town like Kinston."

"So Ethan knew?"

"What? About me being gay?" Marcus laughed. "Yeah, I'd say he knew, Liam."

"So, like . . . I'm sorry for assuming all that stuff about you."

"It's okay. You didn't know."

"Yeah, but I just assumed you were straight, like it was the default."

"That's kind of a larger problem than just you."

"Yeah, but still, I'm sorry."

"It's okay."

"Have you ever dated anyone?"

"Yeah, I have."

"It sounds like it didn't go well."

"It should sound like I don't want to talk about it."

"Oh . . . I'm sorry."

"No—I shouldn't have snapped at you like that. I'm still processing."

"What happened? You don't have to tell me—I'm just being nosy."

"It's okay. We were going to different schools next year. You know I'm going to NYU, right?"

"Yeah. In New York."

"Yes, Liam. New York University *is* in New York." He laughed, but it didn't feel malicious. "And he was staying in North Carolina."

"So you broke up?"

"He decided it. He told me that high school relationships never last past graduation, and that it'd be even harder if we were nine hours away from each other. Then he said there were better men for me in New York."

"Sorry, I didn't mean to bring you down. I've just been thinking about relationships a lot."

"It's okay. Maybe it's good to talk about these things."

"Yeah, maybe. I don't feel better about my friends, though."

"Well, I can't work my magic all the time, Lee."

"Thanks for listening to me, though, Marcus. I do feel better."

"No problem, Liam." Then he paused. "Would you want to get out of the house tomorrow night? I'm meeting with some friends in Goldsboro. You could come with."

"Oh, um . . . yeah, maybe. I'll let you know."

I was doubtful that either of my parents would want me out of the house anytime soon.

But I knew I was going to get out of here anyway.

K nowing that Marcus was gay made things different. *In a good way*, I thought. At least there was someone else I could share my feelings with.

I remembered when I'd told Joel I was nonbinary. The lead-up to that night was tough, and for a long time I'd internalized this bullshit idea that I was just copying him when it came to our trans-ness. I'd been hanging around him too much, or I wanted the attention that he was getting.

But that wasn't it, it was never it, and I doubt that'd ever been the case for any trans or nonbinary person out there. I'd just sat him down, explained how I felt. I thought that he would understand me the most out of any person.

And he did.

He helped me parse out the feelings, explained that he'd felt much the same way before he came out too. Even if our versions of being trans were different from each other, the feelings were still there, the discomforts, the dysphoria. As much as I'd tried to find explanations online, it was so much more helpful to have him there, in front of me, as I explained how I saw my body when I looked in a mirror, how I'd imagined the ways I could change it, how I hated being thought of as a boy.

And of course, Joel hadn't had all the answers, but he'd pointed me toward some resources.

Then I'd cried tears of joy, of relief.

He'd helped me tell Vanessa and to come up with a plan to tell my parents. Funny how he'd helped me figure out so much about myself and yet I didn't know if he was going to be a part of my life anymore.

I snatched the headphones off my head, frustrated with myself. I was supposed to be working on this paper for English, but I couldn't get to the words. I'd been working all day, cycling through whatever music I thought might help me get a groove going.

But there was nothing.

I switched among Charli XCX, Soccer Mommy, Arca, Carly Rae Jepsen, Rico Nasty, all artists who I adored, but at that moment their music felt empty to me. Even the lo-fi hip-hop channel on YouTube didn't spark anything within me.

I was getting tired and feeling really claustrophobic. I'd

been trapped in my room for so long with no one to talk to and nowhere to go. I'd texted Joel and Vanessa, both in the group chat and separately, and yet neither of them had answered, even though they were posting stories on Instagram.

Then I saw that Marcus had posted something to his Instagram.

I thought about texting him, but we'd talked last night, so in my head, it felt weird to take that step back.

He answered after the second ring. "Hey, Liam."

"Hey . . . sorry for calling again."

"Don't keep apologizing. What's going on?"

"I wanted to see if you were still going out?" I looked at the clock in the corner of my computer screen. 5:34 seemed like an appropriate time to go out, right?

"Um, yeah. I was going to text you actually."

"You're sure it's okay with everyone that I'm coming?"

"Well, it's not like I proposed you join us. It's just us hanging out; there's no asking permission or whatever."

"But no one's going to hate me for being there?" I asked.

"No. I'll be there in five."

I slipped into my shoes and made sure to grab my wallet just in case I'd need it for some reason. I raced down the stairs, ready to meet Marcus when he pulled into the driveway.

Mom was sitting at the dinner table, at an angle that I

couldn't possibly notice until it was too late. She didn't even look up when she spoke to me.

"Where are you going?"

"Out."

"I don't think I want you going out tonight. You're staying home."

"I don't want to."

Now she was looking at me. "I'm not asking you, Liam. I'm telling you."

"I don't care," I said.

"Liam Cooper." Her voice shook.

"I don't know when I'll be back. Don't wait up."

Mom was up in an instant, following me to the door. "I am your mother, Liam Cooper. You get back here this instant. Go to your room."

"I'm good."

I knew that I would come to regret this moments later. I didn't like talking to my mother this way; she'd never done anything to hurt me, not on purpose. But I felt like a different person, like someone else was inhabiting my body and I had no control.

I walked out the garage door, down the steps, and to the driveway, where Marcus was waiting for me. Mom stood at the landing, watching my every step. She didn't say anything to me, didn't demand that I get back in the house. She just watched.

"Let's get out of here," I said as I climbed into Marcus's passenger seat.

"Bossy much?"

"Go!" I buckled my seat belt and felt the lurch of Marcus's truck as we backed out onto the street. And just like that, I was free.

"We're going to Goldsboro, right?" I asked.

Marcus nodded.

"What part?"

"We're hanging out at the Walmart."

"You're kidding."

"Well, our options are kind of limited in Goldsboro."

I opened my mouth to make a suggestion, but nowhere else came to mind. Nowhere besides maybe the sports center where you could rent overly expensive roller skates and bowling shoes.

"Kinston has a Walmart," I told him.

"Yeah, but we've been banned from hanging out there."

"Seriously?"

"Yup." Marcus turned up the radio, and we didn't talk again until we reached Goldsboro, a half hour drive. It should've been uncomfortable, but I already felt comfortable around Marcus. Which felt stupid to me, but also made sense. We drove and drove, eventually pulling off at an exit and making our way to the Walmart. We pulled into the parking lot, driving farther and farther off to the side, where a small crowd of cars was all grouped together, people sitting in their seats with the doors open, music playing. Others had taken up space in the beds of their trucks, their feet hanging off the side. Marcus pulled his truck right up to them.

"Here we are."

"Is everyone here from East Lenoir?" I asked, hoping at least a little bit that maybe Ethan's girlfriend would be here.

"Some."

I knew most of their faces from the hallways and from classes, though I didn't know all their names.

"Hey, Thompson!" someone shouted to Marcus. I wasn't sure who.

"You already faded, Jackson?" Marcus replied.

"Maybe a little bit."

I climbed out of the truck.

"Oh shit—you're Ethan's little brother, right?" the guy, apparently named Jackson, asked.

"Yeah."

"Tight."

While there seemed to be small clusters all within the same section of the parking lot, this one seemed like the place to be. It was this truck that was playing loud upbeat country music about a tractor, and the spot that everyone seemed to be drifting toward.

Marcus hoisted himself up into the bed of the truck, stepping on a tire that was nearly half my height and throwing himself over the edge. I tried to copy him, nearly slipping off the tire and busting my lip open. I imagined a world where Marcus would have to lift me back into his truck and take me to the emergency room to get stitches.

"So what's going on here?" a girl asked.

I knew her already. Not well, but I was pretty sure that her name was Kayleigh.

"Liam needed to get out of their house," Marcus said.

"And what makes you think we want to hang out with a sophomore?" another guy asked. This one I didn't know.

"I'm a junior, actually," I said.

"Oh, he speaks!"

For once, I was grateful that I didn't mind he/him pronouns because I really didn't have it in me to explain all the complications of gender with this crowd.

"Well, what's going on with you?" Kayleigh asked Marcus. He sat down slowly, and it dawned on me that there wasn't enough room for me to sit, so I was forced to balance precariously on the side of the truck, hoping that I wouldn't lose my balance and bust my skull open on the asphalt below.

"Nothing," Marcus said.

"Hanging out with your dead best friend's kid brother doesn't seem like nothing."

I watched as Marcus's brows furrowed.

"Don't talk like that."

"Whatever."

"So, Liam . . ." Jackson pulled a pack of cigarettes out of his back pocket, smacking the bottom of the box a few times before he slid one out and balanced it between his teeth. "What's going on with you?"

"Nothing much," I told him.

"I hear that."

I wasn't really sure what he meant by that.

"So . . . is this all you do?" I asked Marcus, not sure if he'd heard me at first.

"What?"

"Sit in a parking lot and smoke?"

"You got anything else better to do?"

"I guess not."

"Are you feeling okay?"

I shrugged. "I guess. I don't know."

I honestly had so many questions for Marcus, ones that I still wanted to ask him, but I didn't want to have the conversation in front of everyone here, didn't want to ask Marcus again about how he'd missed Ethan's funeral, how he hadn't even dared to come by the house, to see my parents. I wanted to know where he'd been, what he'd been doing, how he'd been doing.

I pulled out my phone, spying a few missed messages from Vanessa. A bunch of missed calls from Mom, even more from Dad. I knew that I'd be in so much trouble when I got home, but I didn't care. I couldn't stand being there. Though, if it meant hanging out in a parking lot all night, perhaps I would've been better off at home.

"Hey." Marcus nudged me.

"What?"

"You hungry?"

"Kinda, I guess."

"There's a Cook Out across the parking lot. Do you want to get something?"

"Just the two of us?"

"Do you want to invite these assholes?" He smiled, and I smiled back at him.

I looked around the Walmart parking lot, spied a few of the isolated restaurants and stores, including the abandoned Radio Shack that'd closed six years ago. Then I turned back to the crowd of people in front of me, all piled together and having their own private conversations.

Marcus and I stood up, not catching a single person's attention as we threw our legs over the side and jumped down to the pavement. We began walking toward the Cook Out, the two of us side by side, not saying a word to each other. This Cook Out was a small one, with no real interior besides the kitchen. If you weren't grabbing drive-thru, you had to order at a window and sit outside at one of the red metal picnic tables.

"One medium chocolate shake and an order of fries." Marcus gave his order, then turned to me. "And whatever they want."

"Oh . . . are you sure?" I looked at him.

"Yeah, it's cool."

"Okay." Now I felt the pressure to order a smaller size than what I had been planning to get. At least all the flavors were the same price. "Um, a medium cookies and cream for me, please."

The cashier put the order in, Marcus swiped his card, and we sat down at one of the tables, still not really talking to each other.

Then I started to laugh.

"What's so funny?" Marcus asked me.

"It's nothing," I said, trying to quiet myself.

"No, what made you laugh?"

"I was just thinking about how weird it is that we're hanging out together."

"Is it that weird?" Marcus seemed to think for a moment. "I guess you're right, it is pretty strange."

"We've known each other for forever and yet I don't think we know a thing about each other."

"You know things about me."

"I know you play baseball, I know that you drive a truck; you like chocolate milkshakes; you're gay; you like to write, apparently; and you're going to NYU—" I counted off all those facts with my fingers. "And that's it."

"Come on—there's got to be something else you know about me," he said.

"Oh yeah? If you're an expert, name five things about me."

"You make music; you play the piano; you like *Star Wars*; you have bad driving anxiety; your favorite artist is Charli XCX, whoever that is; and your favorite color is blue."

I stared at him in disbelief.

"Wow, okay . . . color me impressed."

"Ethan talked about you a lot."

And suddenly, things took on a somber tone. We waited in silence, watching as one of the waitresses came from inside the Cook Out and delivered our food to us on a big red tray. "There you boys go. You enjoy now."

"Thanks," Marcus said, taking his shake and fries.

There was more silence as we sat there, sipping milkshakes. Marcus was focused on his, waiting until he got his whipped cream below the lid line so he could pop off the plastic top and dip his fries.

"That's disgusting," I told him.

"What?" He bit off the end he'd dipped.

"What you're doing."

"Have you ever tried it?"

"Well, no, I haven't."

"Then how do you know it's disgusting?" Marcus dipped another french fry and handed it to me. "Try it."

"No."

"Just try it." He pushed the chocolate-dipped monstrosity closer and closer until the weight of the ice cream threatened to break the soggy fried potato.

"Fine." I took it, biting into it with one chomp. Instantly my mouth was filled with the salty-sweet taste, and as it settled along my tongue, I actually found myself wanting more.

"Well?" Marcus eyed me.

"It's good," I whispered.

"What was that?" He cupped his hand around his ear, leaning in closer.

"I said it was good."

"There you go."

"Shut up."

Marcus rolled his eyes, pushing his basket of fries closer to me. "And chocolate milkshakes aren't my favorite, by the way. They're just the best to dip fries in."

"So what *is* your favorite?" I asked him.

"Watermelon."

"Yeah, I don't think that'd taste very good."

"Again, I say don't judge until you've tried."

"Fair enough."

"Meanwhile . . . I'm going to guess that things haven't magically gotten better with your friends in the last twenty-four hours."

"What gave you that idea?"

"Because you're hanging out with me."

"No . . . they haven't." I played with the straw of my milk-shake, contemplating a spoon because both the ice cream and the cookies were so thick that I could hardly get any through the straw. "Do you mind if we talk about something else?"

"Sure, like what?"

"I don't know . . . Why don't you tell me something? Let's get to know each other."

"What do you want to know?"

"Do you have a smart response for everything?"

"Margaret Bright did just barely beat me out for valedictorian."

"Wait . . . seriously?"

"You really have the word *gullible* written on your fore-head, huh?"

"What's that supposed to mean?"

"Gullible, it means—"

"No, I know what gullible means." I picked up a french fry and threw it at him. "Asshole."

"Hey, don't waste valuable potatoes. I bought these."

"Well, if you stopped being an asshole . . ." I didn't know where I was carrying that sentence, so I started a new one. "Are you really going to New York in June?"

"Yeah. I'm hoping I can eventually get into their creative writing program."

"Creative writing." Truth be told, I'd never thought of Marcus as a writer. Not that I didn't think about Marcus often, but when I did, it certainly wasn't whether or not he was a good writer. Suddenly my face felt warm, and I was sure my ears were turning red. "What do you write?"

"Poetry."

"Seriously?"

Marcus dipped another fry. "Is that so surprising to you?"

"A little."

"You need to open your worldview a bit. Get to know people a little more before you assume."

"You sound like a pretentious dickwad."

Marcus smiled. "Good. That'll go well with all the hoity-toities I meet in New York."

"What did Ethan think about it?"

Marcus's smile vanished, and suddenly things felt dour. "About what?"

"The poetry," I said. "The move."

"He liked my poetry. Pushed me to submit my work and apply to NYU."

"That's good."

"He wasn't so happy when I got in, though."

"What do you mean?"

"Something else."

"What?" I asked, confused.

"Something else—let's talk about something else."

"Can I still ask about poetry?"

"Sure, what do you want to know?"

"Who is your favorite poet?"

Marcus finally smiled again. "That's a big question with a bigger answer."

"Top three?"

"Oh yeah, that makes it *soooooo* much easier." He paused, and I thought he was done talking and that things were going to get awkward before he answered, "Ocean Vuong, Sylvia Plath, and Audre Lorde."

"We read a Sylvia Plath poem in English. It was depressing."

"Well, yeah . . . that's why it's so good."

"You're a masochist." I spooned a little bit more milkshake into my mouth. "Do you want to be a poet or whatever?"

Marcus eyed me. "Well, that'd be tough. Writers hardly make any money—even less if you write poetry. So I don't know. I think I want to teach poetry one day, alongside writing it."

"So you'd be a professor?"

He shrugged. "Maybe. What about you? Do you want to do something with your music?"

"I mean . . . that's the goal, isn't it?" I stopped. "But then I think about the money, and if my music is good enough for all that, and I just don't know if I have what it takes."

"Right."

"Besides, my parents want me to do something 'worthwhile.' I doubt going to college for music production or study would be something they consider 'worthwhile.'"

"You never know until you try. They could surprise you."

"Maybe . . . I just don't know. I remember this one time, Ethan told me that I needed to do what made me happy and not to worry about what my parents thought about my art."

"Do you have any of your music on your phone?"

"Do you . . . you want to listen to it?"

"If you'll let me."

I pulled my phone out of my pocket, ignoring the additional texts I'd gotten from Mom and Dad, and pulled up my SoundCloud. I wanted a good song to show Marcus, something that I was proud of. And I knew exactly the song. It was one I'd finished late last year, just before Christmas.

I'd never released it, though. I'd been too scared.

"Here." I hit play and let Marcus take my phone.

I would've preferred for him to have headphones while he listened. I'd used this fake guitar in one of my music programs, and I wasn't sure if he'd be able to pick up on it through just the phone speakers. It'd been tough to learn, but it wasn't like I didn't have the time. I liked how slow it was, how quiet. I'd undercut it with some pops and synths, but I'd wanted the song to be minimalist, different from anything I'd done before.

"Where are the lyrics?" Marcus asked.

"There aren't any."

That was his only question until the song was over. When it ended, he handed the phone back to me.

"I'm not good with words," I said. "Not like you are, apparently."

"Lyrics and poetry are different. Lyrics are like a collaboration with the music, while poetry makes its story all on its own."

"I've just never been good at expressing myself that way."

"Have you tried?"

"What do you think the answer to that is?" I stared at him.

"Now who's being the smartass?" He glared at me, another fry in his hand.

"Vanessa has always been better at lyrics than I am."

"Well, maybe you just need to develop your own talent instead of focusing on hers."

"How?"

"Reading. Studying. Poetry."

"You just said they were different."

"They are. But they're also not."

"What does that even mean?"

He shrugged. "I don't know. I just like fucking with you."

"Okay, asshole."

"Seriously, though—the song is beautiful. You could do something with it."

I felt the heat flood my cheeks. "Do you really think so?"

"Have you released it?"

"No."

"You should. Don't you have followers?"

"Yeah, but—"

"I'm sure they'd like it."

"I want lyrics first."

"You know songs don't *have* to have lyrics, right?"

"You're the one who's pressuring me to write them!"

"Touché."

"Maybe I'll release it." I stared at my screen, at the little lock icon that sat beside the title, the icon that told me that I and I alone had access to this song. Maybe I could release it. Maybe one day, when I wasn't so scared.

We talked a little bit more about music—it *appalled* me that he wasn't a Charli XCX devotee, and he told me about this band called American Football he really loved, and he played me this song they had with Hayley Williams.

When the fries were all gone and the milkshakes a distant, melted memory, Marcus asked me, "Are you ready to go?"

"Yeah, sure."

I followed Marcus back across the parking lot to his truck. A few more people had joined the so-called party—they all cheered for Marcus, some questioning where he'd been, but he ignored them all as he climbed into the driver's seat. The engine turned and we rolled out onto the street. We took turns with the radio, introducing each other to some of our favorites. It was an ideal way to spend a half hour.

"Thanks for tonight," I said when we got to my house.

"You ever need me, just call, okay?"

"Thanks." I felt the weight float off my chest, even just a little bit. I climbed out of the truck and watched as Marcus backed out again, not even waiting until I was inside before he left. Alone, and in the dark, I climbed the steps to the door that led to the kitchen.

"Where were you?" Mom asked as soon as I walked in, not even giving me time to leave my shoes.

"I was out with Marcus."

"Why?"

"Because I needed to get out of here." I tried to step past her, but she was blocking my way. Then Dad appeared.

"Liam, you can't just disappear like that."

"Why not? It's not like either of you care what happens to me."

"Where did you get *that* idea?" Mom asked, her voice sounding so hurt.

"I didn't have to get it from anywhere. It's always been obvious from the way you treated me versus the way you treated Ethan. You can't just start targeting me now that he's gone. That's not fair."

"Liam, we need to talk," Dad said.

"No, I don't want to talk to either of you." I moved around Mom, brushing past Dad so I could finally reach the stairs.

"Liam, we need to discuss your punishment for disobeying us," Dad said.

"I'm tired."

"Liam Cooper!" Dad shouted my name, and it shook me to my very core. My gentle, soft-spoken father yelling my name for what was probably the first time ever. It made me pause. "We understand that things are hard for you right now, but that doesn't excuse this behavior."

I turned on my heel, staring right at the two of them as they looked right back at me, probably not recognizing the person who stood in front of them. The person who looked like their child but certainly wasn't acting like him.

"I don't give a shit what either of you want," I almost shouted at them. "I don't give a fuck!" I stormed up the rest of the stairs, thinking that what I'd said made me sound so cool and powerful.

It was only when I was back in my room that I realized: I didn't feel cool or powerful at all.

monday, april 22, 2019

after

I was dreading Monday.

    I didn't want to see Joel, not after the way that we'd spoken to each other. And I didn't want to see Vanessa simply because I didn't want the reminder that she only seemed to be texting me about music, not about what was really going on. But I had to put my big-boy underwear on . . . because I needed a ride to school.

"Hey," Vanessa said when I got into the back seat. "How was your weekend?"

"Nothing really happened," I told her and Joel. "A fight with my parents, studying for a test I'm probably going to fail. You know, the usual." I didn't mention Marcus; I didn't feel the need to.

"Riiiiiight . . ." Vanessa let her voice trail off.

"Sorry I had to cancel on you, Lee," Joel said. I was glad that he was the one who'd brought it up; I supposed it eased at least a little bit of the tension.

"Yeah, sorry," Vanessa continued. "My dad wanted Joel there."

"We could totally hang out this Friday, if you still want!" Joel added.

"You sure you won't abandon me again?" I asked. That was completely the wrong question to ask, the wrong moment to decide to be snarky.

Joel dropped his head. "Liam, I said I was sorry. But Vanessa really wanted me there. You understand, right?"

I opened my mouth, weighing my options. "Yeah, I understand. Sorry."

Now *I* felt like the one in the wrong.

Vanessa was able to drop me off at home after school.

I offered, "I thought, if you weren't busy, we could work on the EP?"

"Oh . . . um . . ."

It was obvious by the tone of her voice that she didn't want to do this anymore, or at least, not with me. Which was fine; it was totally and completely fine. She was just cutting me off from working with her, something that I was pretty excited to do that she no longer wanted.

"Not today," she told me. "What about tomorrow?"

"Yeah, maybe!" I lied.

We said our goodbyes, and I walked inside. No one was home yet, so I turned my music up as loud as I wanted and I stuffed a pillow over my face, letting out a long guttural yell, grateful that the outro to "Track 10" was covering up any worries our neighbors might have that I was being murdered. I just lay there, on my bed, thinking of all the ways my life was falling apart around me.

I had nothing.

No parents, no brother, no friends, no life outside the music I made.

I stared at my wrist, tracing my veins with my free hand, wondering what I could do to make this all better. But hadn't I tried? I'd tried to stay friends with Joel and Vanessa. I'd tried to get Mom and Dad to understand where I was coming from. I'd tried, and still, none of it had done anything.

So what was the point?

I could be like Ethan, and have my entire life ahead of me, striving for more, to prove myself.

Only to be struck down.

I thought about googling the point of life, but I knew all I'd get were a bunch of posts from Reddit and other forums asking the same question, and I'd have some people saying the point was love, or God, or leaving a mark, whatever that meant, and other people saying that there was no point, that I might as well go ahead and end things while I was thinking ahead. Or wacko conspiracy theorists saying that Russia or China were going to take over the world in ten years so we'd all be dead anyway.

Those weren't the answers that I wanted.

I wanted my own answer.

I wanted something for *me*.

Maybe that was the point.

To live just for me?

I sat up on my bed, moving over to my computer so I could open up GarageBand again. A bunch of files stared at me, songs that were complete but unreleased, other songs that I'd left half-finished, unsure of what to do next.

I opened one of them.

And then I went to Google and typed in *Sylvia Plath poetry*.

Immediately a poem caught my eye.

"Morning Song."

Gold watches and seasons and elements and midwives. It took me reading it three times to understand that it was about a mother going to comfort her newborn child in the night when they started to cry. It made me feel sad, but also wanted;

I couldn't explain it. I wasn't a mother, and would hopefully never be one, but the poem still made me feel close to the feeling of waking up in the middle of a cold night to comfort someone.

I opened up the notes app on my computer, copying a few lines of the poem so I could remember them.

Then I began to write.

saturday, march 16, 2019

H ey!”

Ethan yanked off my headphones, letting them snap back around my head.

"What the fuck?" I stared at him.

"I was shouting for like ten minutes. Why do you listen to your music so loud?"

"'Cause I need to hear it!"

"Well, come on."

"What?"

That's when I noticed the glove and ball in his hand.

"We're going outside. You know, that place you hate so much."

"I don't hate the outside," I muttered, turning back to my computer screen. I'd almost gotten this song figured out—I could feel it. And once I was done, I could send it to Vanessa so she could give me feedback, maybe master it for me, and we could post it on SoundCloud.

"You've been staring at that screen for, like, five hours."

"Yeah, and?"

"It's not healthy. You're going to kill your eyesight."

"You're the one who wears contacts."

"I said come on!"

"Pfft, whatever. I'm almost done with this." I looked at the glove in his hand. "I don't want to play."

Ethan shook his head and reached behind my monitor, pressing the power button at the back.

"What the fuck?" I stood up so quickly that it knocked my chair completely over. "You can't just do that." I reached for the button, pressing it carefully, hoping that he'd only pressed it enough to get the monitor to go to sleep.

Thankfully, my display blinked back on, all my work safe.

"You could've erased an entire day's worth of work I'd done."

"It was just the monitor, Lee. Chill out."

"Shut up. I don't want to play baseball."

"You need to exercise, get out there. Plus I need to practice my pitches, and Dad's busy."

"So? That's not my problem."

"Come on, Lee, you used to love playing catch."

"Yeah, when I was eleven." And before a missed ball from Ethan would knock my teeth out. I didn't think he realized just how dangerous it was playing catch with him. He had a powerful arm that made him vicious with either a ball or a bat. If one of us wasn't careful, I'd end up in the grass with a broken nose and a mouthful of blood.

"I'm good."

"Lee, don't be a pussy."

"Don't call me that."

"What? You gonna get angry? Come on, pussy." Ethan lunged at me with his fist, and I flinched. Which was apparently so funny that it had him in hysterics. "Haha, two for flinching."

Then he punched my shoulder twice.

"Fucking idiot!" I leaped at him, but he was already running down the stairs. I nearly lost my footing following him to the kitchen, where he was waiting for me on the other side of the counter.

When I went one way, he went the other.

For a moment I thought about jumping onto the counter and racing at him, but I figured I lacked the upper-body strength to do that.

"Children!" Mom shouted from the dinner table, where she was looking over the various papers in front of her. "Stop running!"

"He hit me!" I told Mom.

"Well, Lee wouldn't stop working on that noise he calls music to help me practice."

"I told you, get Dad to help you."

"Dad's busy! He told me to come get you."

"Boys, please. Stop. I already have a headache from reading this thing." She lifted up the contract she'd been reading over and editing to show us, not even realizing her mistake. "Lee, help your brother. He needs to practice."

"But I was working on a song, and I'm really close—"

"I don't care," Mom said, looking me straight in the eye. "Ethan needs someone to practice with, and since your father is busy, that's you."

"Why can't you do it?" I asked Mom.

She didn't look at me. She simply sighed and covered her face with her hands. "Please, just do what I say."

"But I was working on a song—"

"And it will still be there when you're done, Liam. Please, just do whatever your brother asks you to do."

I turned back to Ethan, who had the most sanctimonious grin on his face.

"Bullshit," I whispered.

"What did you say, young man?" Mom asked.

"Nothing," I said, my stomach twisting. I didn't even think

she'd realized what she'd said, how she'd called me a "young man" when I'd told her so many times before that I didn't like being called that.

"That's right—nothing. Now get outside. Fresh air will do you some good."

"Come on, Lee," Ethan said, his voice a little more gentle. I followed him outside, and he held the door open for me as if he was sympathetic to what I'd just experienced. It was nothing new, our family's desire to see Ethan soar above and beyond. There were moments that I understood it, and some days when I could even revel in the hype alongside them.

"How long do I have to do this?" I asked as Ethan handed me a worn glove, the one that I always wore when I was forced to do these practices with him.

"I need to get some practice in."

"You keep saying that, but what am I supposed to do?"

"You catch and throw it back to me."

"I'm a terrible catcher."

Ethan threw the ball at me with no warning. I ducked out of the way, barely seeing the ball fly through the air before it landed in our neighbors' backyard.

"Yeah, I know," Ethan said with a grin. "Now go get the ball."

"Asshole," I muttered under my breath.

I ran to retrieve the ball and prepared myself to make the

throw. As awful a catcher as I was, I wasn't a half-bad pitcher. I reared my arm back and threw the ball Ethan's way.

He caught it effortlessly.

"Nice one."

"Thanks," I said. "Now hurry up—I want to finish my song."

"It's just a song—like Mom said, it'll be there when you get back." Ethan threw the ball again. This time, I came close to catching it, but it still fell from my grip, soaring crookedly toward the patio in the backyard.

"I wanted to keep working on it," I told him when I was back in position. "I didn't want to come out here and throw around a ball."

Ethan paused, catching the ball as I threw it back to him. "I mean, I get it."

I scoffed. "No you don't."

"I do, Lee. Trust me."

"All you do is throw a ball around and swing a bat. That's different from creating something. You don't understand."

Ethan threw the ball again. This time, I managed to catch it, wincing as it struck my hand at such a high speed that it actually stung.

"I don't just throw a ball around," Ethan said, his voice making it sound as if he'd actually been offended by what I'd said.

"Yeah, you do, and you're good at it. So why wouldn't you?"

"I like other things."

I threw the ball back, and he caught it with ease. "Yeah, like what?"

"I . . ." He threw his arm back and the ball flew again.

"What?"

"Nothing."

Nothing. Because I knew that baseball was my brother's entire life. Like it was supposed to be. One day he'd be a world-famous baseball player and I'd still be living at home, trying my best to get paid for making music all while I worked some minimum-wage job. That was the expectation for me; that was what Mom and Dad and Ethan had prepared themselves for.

The worst part was that I didn't even think that Mom and Dad would mind if I went nowhere, if I stayed nowhere. They had Ethan; he was their golden ticket. He'd find a wife, have kids, give Mom and Dad the grandkids they'd always wanted, etc., etc. I was much more of a wild card, which they had realized for sure when I told them I wasn't a boy, but not a girl, that I felt like I was neither but sometimes both. Even though they promised that they didn't mind, that they loved me for who I was, and it didn't matter who I loved as long as I was being safe, as if how I felt I wanted to express my gender and who I was attracted to were the same thing.

But I saw their expressions, the loss of a future they'd imagined for me.

Ethan would give them everything they'd ever wanted.

And I'd always be the disappointment.

"That's not fair," Ethan told me. "And you know it."

"What?"

"Saying that I don't have anything." He threw the ball again, and I missed.

"I didn't say that. You have baseball, and that's okay."

"You don't know what you think you know, Lee."

"Oh yeah?"

"Yeah."

I returned the ball and Ethan threw it again, harder than ever this time. I watched as it soared past me, past the patio, again toward our neighbors' yard.

I turned to Ethan once it had landed. "Seriously?"

"Go get it." He waved me off, kicking the grass underneath his feet.

I did as I was told and sprinted to get the ball, listening to the cars as they drove by on the street nearby. I ran back toward Ethan, staring at the way the sun shone on him, the sweat that had begun to bead on his brow despite the chill of the day.

"What if I told you I hated baseball?" he said from across the yard.

"I wouldn't believe you."

"Why not?"

"Because you love baseball."

He'd been playing for years now, starting in elementary

school. He was on every school's team and played in summer leagues during the breaks. He always watched the games with Dad, and the one time we went to Atlanta for a family vacation, we spent most of that trip at a Braves game, all for Ethan and Dad.

"Do I?"

"I mean . . . yeah?"

"Is that what you think?"

"It's what I know." I threw the ball back to him, and for the first time in I don't know how long, he missed. The ball breezed past his hand, landing in the grass behind him.

We both stood there for a moment, as if Ethan thought that I hadn't thrown the ball just yet, and he was still waiting for me.

"Well," I said, "go get the ball."

That was when we were both surprised by the sound of a car pulling up the driveway.

Marcus was here.

His red truck parked behind Ethan's car.

"Are we done?" I asked Ethan.

"What?"

"Can't Marcus help you practice?"

"Yeah, yeah," Ethan said. "You can go finish your song or whatever."

"Thanks." I took off my glove, tossing it onto the grass and walking back inside. I was gross and sweaty, and thought about taking a quick shower, but there was this hook in my head that I'd thought about on my way back upstairs, and I wanted to get it down before I forgot.

Behind me, before I closed my own door, I heard the back door opening again, and two sets of footsteps. Mom said hello to Marcus, and he and Ethan started to walk upstairs.

I closed my door before they noticed that I'd been listening.

Not that I cared.

I didn't.

This was the way things went. I was someone to Ethan until Marcus came around, and then I was nobody. Which was exactly how I liked it.

friday, april 26, 2019

after

"Hey, so I'm thinking we could hang out at my place tonight," Joel offered while we sat in history that following Friday. "I can make last week up to you. Vee can't come over tonight, so I'll be alone."

"Vanessa's not going to be there?"

"Nah, something about her dad wanting quality time." Joel rolled his eyes.

"I mean, that sounds great."

"Yeah?"

"Yeah."

After school, I followed Joel to his car. He stopped to give Vanessa goodbye kisses, of course. When I was finally free of the spectator hell of their relationship, we drove to Joel's house.

We walked in through the back door, leaving our shoes on the shoe rack in the kitchen.

"Hey, Ma!" Joel called out.

"Hello, con! Hôm nay học có vui không?"

"Mhmm, it was good! Oh, má ơi Liam tới chơi với con."

They both spoke with what Joel had told me was a "southern Vietnamese dialect with a northern accent." One summer, Joel had spent weeks trying to teach both Vanessa and me Vietnamese. Vanessa was better at speaking it than me, but not by much. Apparently my accent was all over the place, and I could never get the diacritics down.

Joel's mom walked in from down the hallway. "Oh, Liam, it's good to see you again," she said with a smile. "How have you been?"

"Fine, Mrs. Trinh. How are you doing?"

"Good, good. Do you two want something to eat?"

"Maybe later, Ma." Joel shot me a glance. I didn't tell him that I was pretty hungry and could've gone for something. "Con và Liam đi vô phòng nhé."

"Okay, I have my card game tonight with my girls. Dinner is on the oven; let it sit for a bit longer. So I'll start dinner for you two."

"Thanks, Ma!" Joel nodded my way. "Come on—I want to kick your ass in Tetris."

"You say that like I don't wipe the floor with you every single time."

We raced up the stairs to Joel's room, leaping onto his bed. Joel reached for the controllers for his Switch, handed me his spare set of Joy-Cons, and booted up the game. An hour later, we were deep in the Tetris trenches. If we each played carefully, our matches could last fifteen to twenty minutes. As the music got faster and the pressure increased, my palms got a little sweatier. I beat Joel, three to two.

"Best four out of six?"

"Nah, I'm tired," I said, handing him my controller and crawling back on the bed. "You play, I'll watch."

I grabbed one of Joel's pillows, bracing my head against the wall as I observed the descent into madness. When Joel got into his gaming mode, he was a monster who no one could stop. Tetris was his biggest weakness, and the competitive version of Tetris only made things worse.

I watched as Joel played round after round, sometimes getting knocked out first, sometimes getting into the top ten only to be beat moments later. He hated it, and yet he was totally addicted to playing.

"Ah, come on! What was that?" I saw Joel consider throwing the controller to the floor before he realized how expensive that mistake would be.

"You should take a break," I told him. "Mostly because I'm hungry."

"One more round."

I rolled my eyes, groaning. "Okay."

Joel started up a new round, waiting for the ninety-nine other players to connect before the game started. Then Joel went wild. He leaned in close to the small television in his room, his back bent at an unnatural angle as if it made him a better player. I listened to the click of the controls as he pressed buttons at speeds too fast for me to even comprehend. I watched as his pieces turned and slid into place, as other competitors made combos that clogged up Joel's play area with gray blocks. But Joel was always there to counter it.

He got caught up in the winning, and eventually I moved off his bed, walking down the hallway to the kitchen. Even from across the room I could smell the pot that had been left on the stove to simmer, and I was pleasantly surprised when I lifted the lid and found thịt heo kho, one of my and Joel's favorite dishes.

The pork belly had been left to simmer for what must've been hours, and the caramelized eggs floated with the broth. I was never one for soups—I'd just never found one that I liked—but any broth that Mrs. Trinh made got my mouth to water. I grabbed two bowls from the cabinet above the sink and filled them up with as much of the pork belly as I could. Then I grabbed some blanched spinach for myself since Joel had an aversion to almost anything green or vegetable-like, much to his mother's dismay.

I tiptoed carefully down the hallway back to Joel's room, making sure I didn't spill a drop of the broth on the floor. Mrs. Trinh would kill the both of us if she found out that we'd eaten anywhere besides the kitchen.

And as I got closer to Joel's door, I heard him talking to someone.

"Yeah, I won! Finally," he said. "You should've been here to see it."

I obviously couldn't tell who he was talking to, but I figured that it had to be Vanessa.

"Well, I'll just have to win next time you're here, huh?"

Another pause.

"Oh, really? That sucks." Joel's tone suddenly turned to one of concern rather than flirtation. "Well, you could always come over here. My mom made dinner before she left."

Seriously? He was inviting Vanessa to our night together?

"Yeah, they're here," Joel said. My blood froze.

Another pause.

"Fine, I guess. A little pissy."

He *was* talking about me.

"Yeah, better than they have been, I guess. Still a little weird. No, they're getting food now, so I think we're safe."

Pause.

"I know, Vee, I know. Liam *is* going through a lot, though."

Another pause.

"Yeah, I know; it's draining."

Pause.

"Yeah, yeah. I promise. So you're coming over?"

Pause.

"Okay, and hey—maybe we can take Liam home early? They're not even playing—they're just watching. My mom won't be back until late, and we could have some alone time?"

I closed my eyes, trying to breathe as it felt like the world was closing in around me. I didn't know what to do with the confirmation that my only two friends in the world hated being around me. That was it, wasn't it? They'd said these things to each other in private, hoping that I wouldn't be able to hear them. For a moment I thought about walking back into Joel's room, giving him his food, behaving normally, as if my entire world hadn't just been upended once again. But I didn't. Instead, I walked back to the kitchen, leaving the bowls of cooling food on the counter.

I thought about calling my parents to come and pick me up, but would they be willing after all the things I'd said to them? I stared at my phone, knowing that Dad would be more sympathetic to me than Mom would, but when I hit dial for his number, it rang and it rang and then went to voicemail.

"Fuck," I muttered to myself.

"Hey, Liam, everything okay?" I heard Joel call from his room.

"Yeah!" I shouted back.

I called Dad one last time, but it went to voicemail again, and for a moment I pictured Dad lying on the ground, dead. Or maybe he'd had a heart attack at his desk at work and no one had found him yet. I knew that these scenarios weren't true, I knew that, and yet my mind still wandered toward those possibilities.

I hit dial again, my palms getting sweatier with each passing second. This time there was an answer.

"Liam?" Mom's voice echoed in my ear.

But I didn't register that it was her. "Dad, please. You're alive."

"Liam, honey? Are you okay?"

"Mom?" I pulled the phone away from my face and stared at the screen. There was Mom's name right above the other options I had during this call. "Mommy."

"Liam, are you okay? You sound strange."

"Can you come get me from Joel's house? Please."

"Of course. honey. Is everything all right?"

"No, it's not. I—I—" I stammered through my words, unsure of what to tell her. "I don't want to talk about it right now."

"I'm on my way. You just wait there, okay?"

"I will."

I hung up first, leaving my phone on the counter while I wiped at my eyes. Why did my brain seem so dark? Why did Joel's words keep echoing in my mind? What was happening to me?

The door in Joel's kitchen opened, and Vanessa strolled in, not even seeing me at first.

"Joel! Liam! I'm here!" she called. She slipped her shoes off, leaving them on the shoe rack. And then I heard Joel coming down the hallway, his steps echoing off the wall.

"Hey, Lee—" He paused.

And then I felt a hand on me.

"Liam? Are you okay? You're shaking."

I turned slowly, facing Vanessa and Joel, who were now hanging over me, staring at me. I glanced down at my hands, and Vanessa was right, they were shaking. Not even subtly; I could see each movement, each vibration.

"What's happening?" I asked the both of them.

"Liam, are you okay?"

"No, I—" I looked up at them. "Just . . . I just . . . just leave me alone."

"What?" Vanessa stared at me.

"I said leave me alone."

"Liam, what's going on? Are you okay?" Joel knelt down with me to the floor.

"You just need to breathe," Vanessa told me, taking my hand in hers. "Okay, remember last time, match my breathing or else you might hyperventilate."

"No." I yanked my hand back. "Just get away from me!"

"Liam, what's wrong with you?" Joel stared at me, getting in closer.

"I said get away!" I stood up quickly, knocking Joel over to the floor. It took a second for me to realize everything happening around me, letting it sink in slowly. "Just leave me alone."

"What is your problem?" Vanessa stared at me, shocked.

"My problem?" I looked at her, and then at Joel. "I heard the phone conversation. I heard you two saying how much of a downer I was, how you wanted to get rid of me because you wanted alone time or whatever, and how you don't like being around me."

"Lee—" Vanessa's gaze softened, and she took a step back, raking her hands through her hair. "We didn't say that stuff."

"I heard Joel talking to you," I said.

"We didn't say that stuff, I promise," Vanessa said, but her eyes suddenly couldn't find my own for more than a beat.

"Then what did you say?" I asked her. "*What did you say?*"

"None of that."

"Then tell me."

She looked at Joel, and Joel simply stared at her. He'd picked himself up slowly, leaning against the counter like he didn't have a dog in this fight, as if he'd been innocent.

"I knew this was going to happen," he said, shaking his head.

"Why do you two hate me all of a sudden?" I asked them.

"We don't hate you," Vanessa said.

"You think I haven't noticed the way you two act around me now? How you ignore me, make plans without me? And whenever you *do* invite me somewhere, you're always so far up each other's asses that I might as well be alone."

"We're dating, Liam," Vanessa said. "We want to spend time with each other."

"*I know,*" I said, wiping at my eyes. "But you two were my best friends, and now you act like I don't exist, and you keep abandoning me and that doesn't feel good. *Especially* now."

"Lee—" Joel tried to step in, but I stopped him.

"You." I pointed. "I heard you on the phone, talking about getting me to go home so that you and Vanessa could be alone. I know what I heard. So you two can't even stand the idea of hanging out with the three of us? It's either you two or nothing."

"You know what, Lee?" Vanessa looked at me, her arms crossed. "Yeah, we're a little sick of you."

"Vanessa," Joel cut in, his tone harsh.

"No, I'm telling them," she said, and Joel made no effort to stop her. "We know it's a hard time. We want to be there for you. But any time we reach out, you just tell us you're okay and that you don't want to talk about it. We *try*, but you bottle everything up."

I stared at her, not believing what I was hearing. "My brother died."

"We get that, Liam. We understand that—"

"No, you don't—you fucking don't. You don't understand what that's like. And I'm sorry if I've been draining to be around, but I've been going through a lot, okay?"

"We know," Joel said.

"It's been a month, you guys. I can't just be over this. Don't you think I would be if I could?"

"We're not mind readers," Vanessa said. "The only way we're going to know this is if you tell us. And you've been silent, Liam. Absolutely silent. And there's nothing we can do with that."

I looked at Joel. "You feel this way too, huh?"

He didn't say anything, didn't look at me. He just kept his mouth shut and his eyes on the floor.

"Fine, then I guess you don't have to worry about me anymore. Consider yourselves no longer responsible."

"Liam, you know that's not how we meant this," Vanessa said.

"No, I know how you meant it. You're going to regret this when you two break up. When neither of you have anyone to run crying to."

"We're not going to break up," she said.

"Oh please—you two are sixteen. You think this is going to last?"

"We're planning on it," Joel told me, and I could see the hurt in his eyes.

"Well, it's not, and you two are giving me up for it. How's that feel?"

"Oh, shut the fuck up, Liam," Vanessa said. "Seriously. You don't know what you're talking about."

"I know enough. Enough to know that you two are going to have some huge argument and this will all be over, probably soon."

Just then, through the small window above the sink, I could see Mom pull into Joel's driveway.

"I'm leaving," I said, grabbing my shoes, not even bothering to put them on before I raced outside.

"Liam," Mom said as I got into the passenger seat. It seemed like she'd been prepared to run inside because she was unbuckling her seat belt as I was buckling mine. "Honey, is everything okay?"

"Yes."

"Did something happen?"

"I don't want to talk about it, Mom. Please." I tried my best to hide my face from her. "Can we just go home?"

"Yeah, of course," she said, sounding exasperated. The car lurched into reverse, and we backed out of the driveway. I stared at Joel's house, a place I'd known for over a decade. Spending afternoons and nights over there, playing video games with Joel, eating the delicious food his mom had prepared. The place had almost felt like a second home to me, and I'd always figured it'd be there, even when my own house didn't feel like a place that I belonged. But now it was clear to me, I didn't belong anywhere; there was nowhere for me to go. No friends for me to talk to, no parents who wanted to understand me. There was nothing for me.

Nothing.

after

I spent almost that entire weekend in my room.

I didn't dare leave, not until I noticed late Saturday night that Mom and Dad were both walking out to Mom's car. One of them had knocked on my door about ten minutes before, but I hadn't answered, burying myself under my sheets in case they had something to undo the lock on my door.

When they were both gone, I walked down to the kitchen and grabbed some food, heating up leftover pizza in the microwave and grabbing some chips to snack on when my appetite eventually came back.

I didn't belong in this house anymore, and I hated that feeling. It was almost like I didn't have a place to be.

I thought about texting Marcus, seeing if he'd like to come

and pick me up, but we weren't friends. It was hard to feel like we were anything more than people sharing a tragedy.

Then there were the times I wanted to pick up the phone to talk to Vanessa and Joel. Once I'd gotten as far as to our group chat, which had remained untouched since we'd last used it on Thursday. Joel had sent a pretty fucked-up meme of Sonic the Hedgehog's feet. I still laughed as I read over the caption and my and Vanessa's reactions.

I didn't know what the next day was going to bring, if I'd still have friends come the end of Monday. Dwelling on it certainly didn't solve my depressive episode, but I couldn't help it.

Maybe this was how things were supposed to happen. For days after Ethan's funeral, people kept telling me that everything happened for a reason. Was this happening for a reason?

I tried to spend most of my weekend sleeping.

Late Sunday, I was sitting at my computer, listening to this one song and mindlessly scrolling through a producer forum on Reddit for ideas when a knock came on my door.

"Liam?" It was Dad.

I didn't respond to him, knowing that he was probably trying to get me to come down to dinner for the first time in four days.

"Liam, I know you're in there."

"You don't know that," I said, switching off my speaker in exchange for my earbuds.

"Come on, Lee, open the door. Please?"

"I'm good," I said.

"Liam Cooper, open this door right now." Dad's voice rang so loud that I could hear him over my music. I watched the door carefully, expecting that the sheer power of his voice had magically unlocked it.

I didn't want to talk with either of them, and I certainly didn't want to hear what they had to say about the events of the last few days.

But I stood up and in one fluid motion unlocked the door and sat back down in my desk chair.

"Oh, so that's what you look like," Dad said. "I'd almost forgotten."

"Funny," I said, moving to put my headphones back on.

"No, don't do that. Leave those things off and just listen to me."

"I was working on something."

"Yeah, well . . . now we're talking." Dad closed the door behind him as he moved toward my bed. "I'm asking you to listen, just for five minutes."

"And if I don't want to?" I spared a glance at him.

Dad pointed a finger at me. "You're my child, and you're going to listen to me for five goddamn minutes."

As I met his gaze, I felt like I saw so much of what he was feeling: the frustration, the anger, the fear, the sadness.

Dad leaned back. "I'm sorry, Liam. I'm sorry I yelled at you.

I'm at my end here. You won't talk to us, you're clearly upset, and we've gotten calls from your teachers saying that you aren't paying attention in class or doing your work."

"I'm sorry."

Dad waved his hand. "I'm not here to get an apology."

"Then what are you here for?"

"I'm here to talk to you about what's going on. This isn't something you should be navigating alone. You have us worried, Liam. You're scaring your mother and me."

The words sank into my skin. I gripped the arms of my chair so hard that I was sure the shapes of my fingernails digging into the faux leather would never go away.

"I'm sorry."

"Like I said, Liam, I'm not here for an apology from you, and I don't want to lecture you either." Dad sighed. "As much as we hate it, we do understand what you're going through—"

"You really don't, Dad."

Dad stopped himself, looking off into the corner of my room, as if Mom or Ethan were standing there, helping him to have this conversation.

"Maybe you're right. We don't." He sighed again. "I never lost any of my brothers as young as you did, and then . . . I'm guessing you dealing with all this trans stuff hasn't been easy either."

That made me laugh, mostly to myself.

A sad, pitiful laugh because I didn't know what else to do.

"'Trans stuff,' Dad?"

"Sorry, I don't know all the lingo you kids have. We didn't talk about this stuff when I was growing up. You're actually pretty lucky, you know that? Growing up in a time when all this is being discussed, talked about. When I was your age, we never could've conceived of any of it."

"There were trans and nonbinary people when you were growing up Dad," I told him. I knew that for a fact because of my research, because I'd looked up trans and nonbinary people throughout history, to see how the word had come to be, and how its meaning had been shaped over time. "It's just that they were in the closet, more afraid than we are now."

"I know," he said, shaky again. "I know."

"I'm fine with being nonbinary," I told him. "I'm not worried or confused about that."

"Okay."

"It's Ethan," I said. "And it's you and Mom. It's Joel and Vanessa. It's all those kids at school. It's Marcus. It's everything."

"Did something happen? With your friends?"

"No," I lied, because that was easier in the moment.

"Okay," Dad said, and I didn't think that he actually believed me. "I'm always here, Lee."

"I know, Dad."

"Now can I say something?"

"Sure."

"Your mother and I . . ." Dad took a deep breath, then let it out. "We're trying our best, Lee. This is hard for us too—almost too much to bear. Most mornings I wake up, and I'm not sure what to do with myself, knowing that he's gone and nothing can bring him back. And I only feel worse knowing you're going through this, and I can't help you when we don't know where you are, when we can't sleep at night because we're so worried about you."

I turned away.

"We're trying our best," Dad continued. "There's no guide for this. I mean—there are guides, and we're trying to read them. But they don't make sense. Nothing makes sense because this doesn't make sense. I never imagined we'd lose either of you. *Never.*"

I opened my mouth to say something, but I didn't have the words to convey the confusion and sadness that ran through my mind.

"I never considered that I'd ever have to bury either of you." Dad sniffled, wiping his eyes. "That's all that I wanted to say, Lee. That's it. I just wanted you to know that your mother and I—" Dad stopped himself again. "We are trying. We're trying, Lee. Please, just know that. Whatever we're doing, right or wrong, we're trying our best. We just haven't been left with much to work with."

"I know, Dad."

Did I, though? After the way that I'd yelled at both of them, ignored their pleas, hurt myself in retaliation for a lifetime of being ignored in favor of Ethan and his loves and hobbies and attentions.

I watched Dad as he stood up slowly. "Well, dinner is ready, if you want to come down and eat. And, um . . . Liam? Can you do me a favor? Apologize to your mom, please? Her feelings are hurt, and she misses you."

I stared at Dad, weighing my words carefully. I missed Mom too. I missed talking with her and Dad. I missed family dinners and movie nights, and going to the grocery store with Mom and helping Dad with projects around the house even when I didn't want to. I missed these things that had died along with Ethan.

"I will, Dad." I turned back to my computer.

"Thank you." Dad breathed a sigh of relief, and for the first time during this entire conversation, he actually seemed lighter, almost like the Dad I used to know.

Before.

"Come down if you get hungry." Dad placed his hand on my doorknob and moved to close the door behind him.

"Dad—" I said a little louder than I meant to.

"Yeah?" He peeked his head back in.

I paused, studying him, trying to steady my own self. "You can leave the door open."

Dad looked at me, and I swore I saw the slightest of smiles, or maybe I didn't. Maybe it was something that I just made up to make myself feel better. Either way, I felt lighter too.

"Okay" was all he said before he disappeared down the hallway. I listened to his footsteps as he made his way back downstairs. I didn't follow him; I didn't join them for dinner because it still felt like a foreign place to me, an incomplete place.

No, I stayed in my room, working on my music, my headphones blasting with the beats and synths that I'd spent time creating, only for me to threaten to trash the entire project because I didn't like what I was making. I didn't like any of it, and I didn't want to hear it anymore.

I didn't say good night to either of them, though I did slyly text Dad to see if he'd be willing to take me to school in the morning.

That was the best I could do. My shattered, lost best.

monday, april 29, 2019

D ad woke me up the next morning. A solid hour and a half before my alarm was set to go off.

I heard his voice from somewhere. My eyes were still closed, and I was dreading the day ahead and hoping that it was actually some very real-feeling dream instead of real life.

"Hey, buddy." Dad poked his head in past my door. "You up?"

"Now I am." I rolled over.

"Go ahead and jump in the shower. I want to make a stop before I drop you off."

"Where do you have to be?" I asked.

"Just somewhere."

I showered quickly, dressed even quicker, not caring about how I looked. I was pretty sure I'd worn these pants for the last five days in a row, and I picked the one sweater I had that didn't

214

smell weird. My hair fell to my forehead, covering my eyebrows, and I had two fresh zits on my face.

"Perfect," I muttered to myself.

"You ready?" Dad's voice nearly made me leap out of my skin.

"Huh?" I asked, trying to calm my heart. I eventually processed his question. "Yeah, I'm ready."

"Did I scare you?"

"No, no." I shook my head, pushing my hair out of my face.

"Maybe time for a haircut?"

"Maybe," I answered, grabbing my backpack and following him out the door. Mom was long gone, so there was no awkwardness to avoid. Well, none other than the residual awkwardness I had with Dad. "Where are we going again?"

"It's still a surprise."

The car pulled out onto the street, and Dad started driving in the very opposite direction of school. I pictured this horrific scenario where he was taking me to a hospital, where I'd be strapped down and my brain would be electrocuted until I couldn't see the color blue or something.

But my parents wouldn't do that.

I knew that.

I was still anxious.

Dad drove farther into Kinston, the downtown area that he constantly told us used to be way more popular than it was now.

When he turned down King Street I figured out where we were going. After a few more stops at some lights, we parked in the lot next to Byrd's Restaurant.

"Here?" We'd come here before Ethan's Little League games, or sometimes just on random Saturdays when we wanted to get out of the house.

I loved it.

I could still taste the too-sweet tea and the home fries and the bacon, egg, and cheese sandwiches with just a touch of hot sauce on them.

I looked back at Dad.

"Why?" I asked.

"Does there really have to be a reason?"

"I guess not." I paused. "We just haven't been here in forever."

Dad opened his door slowly, letting us both sit there for a spare moment. "Are you hungry?"

"Starving," I said with a smile.

The food almost felt like home. Walking inside, the restaurant hadn't changed a bit since we were last here, and neither had the food. As I scooped the last bit of my eggs up with my piece of toast, I felt warmed.

Dad sat across from me, finishing off his grits with way too much butter in them. He'd winked at me when I shot him a glance. Mom was always worried about his cholesterol.

"Are you sure there was no ulterior motive in bringing me here?" I asked when I'd swallowed my last bites, washing it all down with sweet tea that probably wasn't a good idea at six thirty in the morning.

"What motive would there be?"

"I don't know, to distract me." I moved my glass along the condensation that had pooled on the table, letting it slide an inch before I grabbed it again.

"Well . . ." Dad wiped his mouth with his napkin. "There is one thing."

"I knew it." I slumped back in my seat, waiting for Dad to say whatever it was that he had to say.

"It's nothing bad, Liam. I promise. I just wanted to run an idea by you, see what you thought of it. Your mother and I have been talking, and we think it might be a good idea for you to go to counseling."

I didn't know how to react.

"With us," Dad continued. "Your mother and I—we've decided to start seeing this doctor in Greenville, and we think that she's going to be a real help with processing everything."

"So you want me to go to therapy?"

"It's more like grief counseling. Our first appointment is next week, and we'd like you to go with us. To speak with her."

"What if I don't want to?"

"Well, we aren't going to force you, but we thought we'd extend the invitation. We've talked with her a bit already and figured out how the appointments will work with all three of us in there at once. She even offered for each of us to get individual time if needed, so you won't have to speak to her with us in the room, if that's a concern."

Were Mom and Dad so scared of me that they were worried about what I'd say in front of them?

I looked at Dad and then back to the table. "I'll think about it."

"Thank you. That's all I wanted you to do."

"Okay. You didn't have to lie to me, though, to get me here to talk about it. We could have discussed it at home."

"I wasn't lying to you, Lee." Dad reached across the table, covering my free hand with his own. "I did just want to have a nice morning with you."

I didn't meet Dad's gaze. Instead, I focused back on my glass.

"It's been a while since we had one," I told him.

"Yeah." Dad paused. "It has."

When breakfast was done, and it dawned on me that I still had an entire day's worth of school left to deal with, the food turned in my stomach. I thought about what I was going to have to say to Joel, and to Vanessa, and how everything was going to happen.

I didn't want to deal with it all.

Dad wouldn't let me skip, though—that much I knew.

As Dad pulled in through the carpool lane, I unbuckled my seat belt. But still I sat there, staring at the front entrance of the school, as my classmates gathered there.

"You okay?" Dad asked.

"Yeah, yeah. Can you pick me up today?"

"Oh, can Vanessa not do it?"

"No, she, um . . . she's out sick today."

"Okay, yeah. I'll leave work early."

"Thanks." I grabbed my backpack and hopped out of the car. Dad waved bye, and I waved back. Once I was inside, it felt like a clock somewhere started, the timer to the big explosion that was going to end my friendships.

I didn't go to the cafeteria.

The whole day, I sat through class, taking my notes, actually trying. It's not like there was some magic cure for all this, but I didn't want anyone calling my parents anymore, saying my work had fallen off.

Mr. Wang ended class right on time, giving us a chance to pack our things before the bell rang. There were a few spare seconds as Vanessa and I both walked toward the door, where we nearly collided with each other. I took a step back, and she looked at me and I let her go.

That was that.

She didn't want to talk to me. We didn't have a big fight in the hallway. There was nothing left to say, I suppose.

after

Dad kept taking me to school, and our morning trips to Byrd's became a ritual, which felt like a step in the right direction. I still hadn't apologized to Mom; I didn't know when I was going to do that. I had to find the courage.

Dad didn't bring it up. No, in my mind, it was Ethan who told me I needed to get on it, needed to do right by my parents. I knew he wasn't actually talking to me, but on some level it felt like he was still there, beside me, in the same room as me, watching me. He was a ghost, following me wherever I went, even when I didn't want him there.

I also hadn't come to a decision on whether or not I was going to join my parents in their therapy session, and considering that it was the next day, my time was running out.

It was hard to avoid the two of them.

Avoiding Vanessa and Joel was much easier, though.

I only had two classes with each of them. I just had to not talk to them. I'd hear Joel or Vanessa laugh; I'd watch as they shared a smile or a soft touch during their free moments. I thought about hiding during lunch, but I was so hungry after a single day of escaping to the library that I went to the cafeteria . . . and immediately regretted it after I'd paid for my food.

This deep into the school year, the seating arrangements had been set, and no one was moving. There were a few free spaces here and there, but I was worried that I wouldn't be granted permission to sit at these tables. Which was ridiculous, but a lot of what happened in high school was ridiculous. So I didn't take any of those empty seats. No, instead I walked out to the senior area, this place just outside the cafeteria where carpentry students had built these picnic tables. I wasn't allowed to sit out here, not without another senior.

But thankfully, there was already someone out there who knew me.

"Marcus!" I said his name from across the yard as I walked down the short steps to the patio. He was in the middle of talking to someone I didn't recognize.

"Liam? What are you doing out here?" he asked.

"Aren't you a junior?" the girl asked me.

I didn't let it bother me that I wasn't welcome here. I just took my seat across from Marcus. "I didn't have anywhere else to go."

"You can't sit here," the girl said.

"Amy." Marcus shot her a glance. "It's okay. He's Ethan's little brother."

"Oh." She looked back at me with more sympathy in her eyes. "Sorry."

"It's okay," I tell her.

"Do you mind giving us some privacy?" Marcus asks.

"Yeah, sure," Amy said, and she turned around and joined the crowd at the other table, which didn't grant *much* privacy, mind you, but their conversation seemed deep enough that none of them even bothered to pay attention to what we were doing.

"What's up?" Marcus asked.

"I didn't have anywhere—"

"No, I heard you the first time. I meant, like, did something happen, or . . ."

"Um . . . well, kind of." I held my hands under the table, gripping myself tightly. "Things kind of came to a head Friday night. With Joel and Vanessa."

"Ah, I see. So what happened?"

"We had a fight."

"Bad enough to ruin a friendship?"

I nodded.

"That sucks. Are you going to talk to them?"

"I don't know. They don't seem very interested in talking to me."

"So you're okay with the friendship ending? You're just done?"

"After the way they talked about me . . . yeah, I think I'm done."

"Huh."

"Huh?"

Marcus just looked at me and repeated himself. "Huh."

"I hate you sometimes."

"Well, join the club."

"What have you been doing?"

"Studying, writing."

"Yeah?" I perked up. "Have you written anything good?"

"Have you?"

"I've been trying," I told him. "I read some of the poetry you told me you liked."

"And?" Marcus said, seeming much more excited than he had seconds before. "What did you think?"

"Some of it was confusing. Some of the metaphors are too deep, I think."

"Ah, Liam, you're killing me here."

"What?"

"Sometimes it's not about the words. I mean, it is, but it isn't always about their precise meaning."

"I don't get it."

"Sometimes it's more about the emotion." Marcus reached

into his backpack and whipped out a huge book with the title *The Complete Poems of Emily Dickinson* on the front.

"You're reading that?"

"Bits and pieces."

"Jesus."

"Sometimes poetry is more about the feeling the words give you, the emotion, the placement, and not necessarily the words themselves."

"But the words are what you read. And you read the words to find the emotion, so the words do matter."

"Okay, now you're just being a dick." Marcus flipped open the book to one of the many pages he'd dog-eared. "Can I read you a favorite?"

"Sure, why not?"

"Don't sound so enthused."

I threw on my most excited voice. "I mean, *oh boy*, I can't *wait* to hear the poetry, Marcus!"

Marcus closed the book. "If I recall, you're the one who wanted to learn more about poetry so you could get better at lyrics."

"Okay, okay," I said, surrendering. "Fine, I'll listen."

"Good." Marcus opened the book again, flipping through pages and pages of text. I could see from here just how many passages he'd highlighted, notes written in the margins of the book, and what looked to be complete poems on pages that had been empty.

I'd believed Marcus liked poetry when he'd said he did—why would that be something someone lied about? But I was beginning to realize just how in love with it Marcus seemed to be.

"Here's one." Marcus looked up at me. "Can I read it to you?"

"Absolutely."

Marcus read me the poem about how hope is a bird or . . . something. Singing and sitting on the soul. It all sounded beautiful, but it went right over my head.

"Wow," I said, not really getting the point of it.

"What does that make you feel?" he asked.

"Um . . . I don't really know. Sad?"

Marcus glared at me. "You aren't taking this seriously."

"I spaced out for most of the poetry unit in English last year."

"Here." Marcus turned the book to face me and slid it my way. "You read it. Read it a few times, and then tell me what it makes you feel."

I looked at the page.

The poem was so much longer than what Marcus read. Hope was a bird again, and it seemed that no matter what the bird was going through, it always remained. Through storms and snow and heat, it was always there.

I read it again, and then a third time.

When I was done, I looked at Marcus and handed the book back.

"So," he asked, "what does the poem tell you?"

"That hope is strong?" I half said, half asked him, hoping that I had the right answer.

"Right." He took the book back. "Do the words make you feel hopeful?"

"Not really," I said. Though *hopeful* wasn't a particularly accessible emotion for me around that time.

"It's the storm," Marcus said. "She's saying that the birds, hope, always sing no matter the weather, which is whatever you're going through."

"I've never heard birds sing during a thunderstorm."

"Perhaps you weren't listening hard enough." He closed the book and slid it toward me. "Here, borrow this for a bit."

I flipped through the pages as they all landed with that satisfying *plop!* that my favorite floppy paperbacks had. "I'm supposed to read all this? This is like a thousand pages."

"It's, like, eight hundred. And they're poems; there's more blank space on the page than actual words. Besides, no one said you had to read it all at once. Digest it slowly; it'll mean more that way."

"Fine, if you think this will help me get better."

"Maybe it will, maybe it won't."

I took the book and eyed it carefully, my fingers tracing over the worn cover, which'd been ripped in places. It was obvious that this was a book that Marcus loved, and he was trusting me with it.

"Hey, um . . ." I still didn't meet his gaze. "Would you want to help me with lyrics? I bet you're really good at them."

He raised an eyebrow. "Isn't that the point of all this?"

"No, I mean . . . like we could collaborate, I guess. You know a lot more about this than I do. We could put our brains together."

Marcus eyed me, and then a slow smile crept up on his face. I felt that familiar thudding in my heart, one that told me I was in trouble. Suddenly, I felt warmer than I had before.

"Yeah, sure," he said.

"Really?"

"Why not?"

"Right . . . um . . . do you think you could give me a ride home, then?"

"Yeah, I can do that."

After school, I went looking for Marcus . . . and found Joel instead. He called out to me and I ignored him, brushing past. I didn't want to keep Marcus waiting, after all.

"Liam, please, wait up!"

I turned to face him. "Oh, so *now* you want to talk to me?"

"I do. I want to talk to you about what's going on." He reached for my hand, his grip tight around my wrist. I tried my best to pull my hand away, but Joel was stronger than me.

"Just five minutes, please," he said.

"Why?"

"Because I want to talk to my best friend, please. I want to talk about what happened."

"You and Vanessa said plenty the other night."

"I don't want to talk about Vanessa. I want it to be you and me; I just want us to talk."

For a moment I wondered if he'd tell me that they'd broken up, all because of the fight, all because of me. I looked at the floor, then at Joel. He was staring at me with his big brown eyes, like he knew what he was doing.

"I've got to go home," I told him.

"Five minutes. Please."

"Fine," I said, knowing that he probably wouldn't let me go until I agreed. "What do you have to say?"

"Let's, um . . ." Joel looked around. "Let's go somewhere less crowded."

We headed to the football field's bleachers. I texted Marcus to say I'd be five minutes, and he told me to take my time, without asking me why I needed it.

Joel took a seat, dropping his backpack. I did the same, sitting a foot or so away from him.

"So . . ." I prompted.

"Sorry, I've just been—I've been thinking."

"Your time is ticking, Joel."

"I'm sorry," he said. "I'm sorry for how things went the other night. I'm sorry for the things you heard. I'm sorry that we said so many cruel things."

"It doesn't matter how many times you apologize," I told him.

"Liam."

"You two *hurt me*, Joel, and maybe if you'd come to me instead of talking about me behind my back, things might've been different. I'm sorry if I was a 'downer' or whatever, but my brother is dead. You don't know what that feels like."

"No, I don't. But I remember when my grandma died, how much it hurt. I remember my mom walking around the house like a ghost; there was a solid week where she didn't talk to me because she was so sad, but then afterward she insisted that she was okay. My grandmother—she hadn't seen me in three years. She died thinking that I was someone else, that I was her granddaughter and not her grandson. This was two years ago and I still think about it all the time; I can't *not* think about her. And I know that it must be harder when it's someone even closer to you. But I *do* understand the experience, if not the magnitude. It is the worst feeling in the world, to know you'll never see someone again, and that they'll never see you."

"I'm sorry, Joel." I didn't know what else to say. "You're right. It's the worst feeling in the world."

"And with Ethan, there are so many things he'll never do. But you can't collapse under the weight of all that."

"Easier said than done."

"I know."

"Look," I said, "if you know all this . . . why did you guys stop wanting to hang out with me?"

"It was getting to be a lot, Liam. Before Ethan. You never seemed happy when you were around us. Specifically because of us. That was a drag. And then, with Ethan—we wanted to be there, but you wouldn't go near talking about it. Which is your right. But you were also ready to jump on us at the drop of a hat . . . and there was no way for us to remedy that."

"You could've told me."

"We didn't know how to," he said. "My therapist says I have pretty heavy anxiety, and then there are the shots, the dysphoria, things with Vanessa and pressures from school, my mom always wanting more from me, the rest of my family and their own opinions on my trans-ness. I didn't know how to talk to you about it, and then, even before Ethan died . . . I don't know, it was just always turning negative around you."

"I can't really control that," I told him.

"I know. We're all going through our shit."

"I'm sorry," I said.

"I'm sorry too."

I was scared of my next words . . . but I still needed to say them. "I don't know if I can be your friend anymore. Not yet anyway."

"Liam—"

"I just don't think any of us should be friends right now. I don't think it's good for us."

Joel paused. "Okay."

"Okay."

Maybe I wanted Joel to fight this, wanted him to beg me to be his friend, to talk to him, to text him. But instead he barely moved as I grabbed my backpack and walked to the student parking lot.

Marcus's truck was still there, sitting idle as he waited for me to join him.

"Sorry," I said. "I got held up."

"It's all right. Are you okay?"

"No, I don't think I am."

"Oh . . . I'm sorry."

"Yeah" was all I said.

Later that night, while I was trying to do my homework and study for the next math quiz, I remembered the book that Marcus had given me. I wanted to do anything except study, but I'd tried to work on a song and I hadn't been able to find the right words, the right beat, the right sound.

It all felt fruitless.

Emily Dickinson weighed my book bag down, making it topple over. I lifted the book out and left it on the side of my desk, telling myself I couldn't open it up yet. But the longer I sat there, the more distracted I was, staring at the spine out of the corner of my eye.

I sighed, closed my textbook, and cleared a spot on the desk so I could open the book wide. I didn't know where to start with this, with poetry. Did it really matter where you began reading?

I opened up to the first pages, with all the copyright information and some history about Emily Dickinson. Then I came to the title page, and right below *The Complete Poems of Emily Dickinson*, there were two words scrawled there in blue pen ink.

For you.

"For you?" I whispered. For who?

Had someone given this book to Marcus? Was it a boyfriend? These two words managed to convey some kind of intimacy that was unfamiliar to me.

Or maybe it was secondhand.

I moved on to the actual poems. I read and read and even reread some. There were those I understood, and there were those I didn't. Actually, most that I read, I didn't understand. I even tried to read Marcus's notes in the margins, and some of them managed to confuse me further.

I huffed in frustration, flipping through pages, breezing through the poems and Marcus's notes, knowing he'd probably cuss me out if he saw me reading this way. I wouldn't even call it reading, I was skimming, I was tired, and I didn't want to do this.

I flipped all the way to the back, where there was even more scrawling in black ink, places that Marcus, or possibly someone else, had written more notes. Then I saw the poems. There were pages of poems, words written in cramped margins.

My eyes settled on one in particular.

Fingers finding lost bodies—
floating along the surface, despaired, drowned, dead.
Keeping secrets lost on pale blue lips—
For this is the place the dead things go—
This is the home of the ghosts we keep.

This was what I thought of when I thought of poetry: melodramatic, depressing. There was no name written at the bottom, no author credited. I selected a few of the words that I saw and plugged them into Google the same way I plugged my own essays in to make sure that my teachers didn't think I was plagiarizing.

There was nothing there.

None of the lines of the poem triggered anything. Which told me one of two things:

Either Marcus had found a super obscure poem and copied it down without crediting the author, or he'd written it himself.

I reread the poem, trying to focus on each and every word like he'd taught me.

Floating along the surface, despaired, drowned, dead.
This is the home of the ghosts we keep.

I didn't know if I was reading too much into it, but this poem felt like it was about Ethan. That's what it made me think of anyway. I read through Marcus's other poems, trying to see if any of them may be related to this one, if there was any other mention of Ethan. But there wasn't. This was the only poem about death as far as I could tell.

I reread the poem one last time. There weren't many words, not enough to make a full song, but I wanted to try something.

I opened up one of my old songs. I didn't want to make a new one for this; I already knew where it'd fit. I had to search through my files for a bit before I finally managed to find the right one, and I let it replay in my ears.

It was sad, somber, quiet.

Different from the music I normally made. It still sounded

good to my own ears, but there were things I wanted to change. I took out the synths, instead replacing them with quieter drumbeats, hoping that would pack more of a punch.

I gave it one more listen before I closed the door to my bedroom, wrapped a blanket up, and stuffed it in the small crack between my door and the floor. I didn't want to run the risk of Mom or Dad hearing me sing.

Then I got out the shitty secondhand microphone I'd bought from Vanessa, not worried about the quality of my voice because I was going to pitch the hell out of it.

And then I sang.

I was not a singer. Not at all. My voice wasn't bad, but even to my own ears it sounded rough.

I got the words down, Marcus's words, and then I added a few of my own, about being angry, being lost, feeling alone.

And I wish that you were here,
But you've left me alone.
Gone off on a journey,
That'll never bring you home.

They came to me, and I hated them, but I'd pause to write them down, to rerecord sections. Eventually, though, I got them all down, and I put them into the song.

I still had to relisten a few dozen times to make sure I was happy with what I'd created, and for the first time in months, I actually was. This song felt like me, it felt like what I was feeling, even if most of it happened to be someone else's words. As I sat there in my desk chair, watching as the clock in the corner of my screen ticked closer and closer to midnight, I started thinking more about it, and the more I thought about it, the worse I felt about the song. Maybe it was too melodramatic, maybe it wasn't upbeat enough, maybe I shouldn't have taken out the synths.

Maybe, maybe, maybe.

Maybe there was more to do with it, maybe I wasn't done, maybe I shouldn't post this anywhere.

But if I never posted it, no one would ever hear it.

The thing was . . . the person I most wanted to hear it would never hear it no matter what I did. This was a song about him, it was *for* him, but he'd never get the chance to hear it.

I saved the file to my desktop and opened up SoundCloud. It was easy to post—just click and drag. SoundCloud had a habit of compressing things a little too harshly for my taste, so I left the song on private and listened to it a few times, fixing anything in the original file that I thought SoundCloud was messing up.

Then I typed in the title.

"Ghosts."

I opened up this copy of Adobe Illustrator that Joel had managed to get for me, and I crudely drew a picture of a ghost with some purple background. I was far from an artist, let alone a digital artist, but I did what I could. And when I was satisfied, I added the artwork to the upload.

Then I hit post.

I didn't expect the song to be big; this wasn't my big break, this wasn't going to make me an overnight sensation. It was a simple song being added to a website with thousands of uploads every single day.

But it was mine, it was my post, and I'd made that with some help.

I went into the credits of the song and made a few changes, making sure to add Marcus's name to the songwriter field.

I listened to it one last time, refreshing as the page crept up from five listens to ten, to thirty, to forty-five. Which was probably average for an hour post-upload.

I turned my computer off, making sure that everything was saved the right way before I crawled into my bed, my body shaking a little from excitement. Despite everything that'd happened that day, and the things I'd said to Joel that still rang in my ears, I still felt the happiest that I'd felt in a long time.

I came up with something."

Those were the first words I said to Marcus the next day. I'd had to wait until lunch to talk to him. My legs had bounced with excitement all day, and I listened to the song again and again during any moment when I was allowed to wear my earbuds. The true test of seeing if you actually liked something that you'd created was to look at it the following morning.

And if you didn't hate it . . . well, then, congratulations.

I hadn't known that feeling all that often.

But this was a song I was in love with, so in love that I was sure I'd dreamed up making it and it was someone else's work that I'd become enamored with. When I checked the credits, though, it was my and Marcus's names staring back at me.

"Okay," Marcus said, setting down the gross-looking cafeteria taco that he'd been about to take a bite of.

"Not here, I don't have my good headphones," I said. "Today, after school."

"Umm . . ." Marcus seemed to think for a moment.

"Oh, come on, you promised."

"I was just thinking. Today should be fine."

"Great, I'll play you the song then," I told him, grateful that I hadn't given Marcus any of my SoundCloud information.

I tried to keep my excitement at bay for the rest of the day, which certainly helped in geography when, after the bell had rung, Mrs. Mills told us to clear our desks of everything except for a pencil that we could circle answers with.

I'd forgotten about the quiz that she'd scheduled. I'd meant to study for it, but I'd gotten so excited about the song last night that it'd completely slipped my mind.

I tried to recall the answers on the paper in front of me, but search as I might, my brain couldn't think of anything. There were some that were obvious, easy right answers that Mrs. Mills had given us, but the further I went into the two-page quiz laid out in front of me, the worse I felt, the more my stomach rolled, and my hand began to shake a little bit.

"Fuck, fuck, fuck." I covered my face with my hands.

Now my legs were shaking for a different reason. There were a few questions that we had to write out longer answers for, and

I couldn't think of the words; then one question asked us to break down cloud formations and I really had to wonder why a geography class of all things was teaching us about clouds and their shapes and what they meant.

"Fuck."

"Liam," Mrs. Mills said from her desk. "Is there a problem?"

"No, Mrs. Mills."

"Well, then, settle down."

"Yes, Mrs. Mills." I dared to look up across the room, where Joel and Vanessa sat beside each other. Vanessa had turned to look my way, turning back when she noticed that I'd caught her. Joel, however, was focused on his test, and only on his test.

Class stretched on, and the closer we got to the bell, the worse the feeling in my head became. I tried to circle any answers I could, write out complete sentences.

"All right, everyone, if you're still working, pencils down. And bring your quizzes up to me."

I looked up at all my classmates, realizing that I was one of two kids who hadn't finished the quiz yet.

"Liam?" Mrs. Mills said, "you still have yours, right?"

Half the eyes in the class looked toward me.

"Yes, ma'am." I stood up slowly, walked to her desk even slower, and held out the paper for her to take. Even by just glancing at it, she could tell what a mess was in front of her.

The rest of the period continued in a blur. All I could think about was how I'd totally bombed that test, and how I was going to fail geography. I'd be in summer school, probably fail that too, and I'd stay a junior while the rest of my classmates moved on without me. I bet Joel and Vanessa would laugh while watching me as I lost it, as I unraveled. I didn't actually believe that, but I couldn't tell my brain otherwise.

I rubbed my sweaty palms on my pants and tried to get my legs to stop shaking.

But no matter how hard I tried, I couldn't.

"Liam." Mrs. Mills's voice shook me to my very core.

I dared to look up at her, at the faces staring at me. She'd been writing something out on the SMART Board when I guess my breakdown had gotten her attention.

"Liam, are you all right?"

"I, um . . ." I spoke quietly, my voice hoarse. "Yeah, I'm okay."

"Do you need to go to the nurse's office?" she asked, concern painting her face.

"Um . . . I . . . no. I'm fine."

What was wrong with me? It was the same feeling I'd had at Joel's house, that same feeling of panic, of hopelessness. I tried to drag myself out of it but couldn't. Finally, the bell rang, and I grabbed my backpack, racing out of the classroom so that I could step outside and feel the May heat on my face. The air helped, but I also stopped in the nearest bathroom, splashing my face with water because that's what people did in the movies when they were stressed—they splashed water on their faces.

"Liam."

I was getting so sick of hearing my name.

I grabbed a paper towel and patted my face dry.

"Liam, are you okay? You looked like you were having a meltdown," Joel said, still standing behind me, almost as if he were keeping guard.

"I'm fine," I lied.

"You don't look fine."

"Yeah, well, it's not like you care anyway." I balled up the paper towel and tossed it into the trash can. "I've got to get to math, don't want to fail."

"We're both going to the same place." Joel stepped in front of me. "We've got plenty of time."

"Just move," I told him.

Joel crossed his arms. "I think you need help, Liam."

"That's old news."

"No, I mean I think you need professional help. I've been through these things I've seen you go through. That fit you had at my house, that seemed like a panic attack. You should talk to a therapist."

"Oh, thanks for the advice." I tried to push past him again, but Joel was too strong for me, too firm to get by. "I thought we'd already had this come-to-Jesus meeting."

"I'm just trying to help."

He stepped to the side, allowing me to try to pull the door open a few times, but it didn't budge.

"Why did you lock it?" I asked him.

"I didn't." He pressed the door with his palm and it opened just fine. "It's push."

"It's push." I mocked his voice, which was probably a step too far, but I couldn't stop myself. "Go to hell, Joel."

"You're being a dick."

"Look in a mirror sometime."

"You need therapy, Liam."

"What I need is people in my life who mind their own damn business." I pushed open the door, letting it swing as far as it'd go before I walked out. My chest heaved, my hands shook, and I felt ready to hit something, or someone.

That wouldn't get me anywhere.

A panic attack? I thought. *What does he know? He doesn't know shit about me.*

I knew the truth, though. I knew Joel was right. He'd talked about them before, the panic attacks he'd had, and as soon as he said the words to me, I'd connected the dots. I just didn't want to admit it. I didn't want to admit that I needed the help. There was so much in my brain, so much that needed unraveling that I most certainly couldn't do on my own. Hell, there was a therapist waiting for me, one provided by my parents, but I just didn't want to admit that I should go.

I thought I could do it on my own.

The day had killed my excitement, even as my body carried me to Marcus's truck, my muscles already remembering the path there. I still felt like shit.

I still had everything Joel said to me stuck in my head.

Panic attack. Therapy. You need help.

I tried to shake those words, but they wouldn't move.

"Hey," Marcus said as I got closer to his truck. He was throwing his backpack into the bed, and mine joined his. "You look like hell."

"Thanks for noticing," I said, climbing into the passenger seat.

"Are you okay?"

"Yeah, just kind of a rough day."

"Do you still want to work on lyrics?"

"As long as you're up for it."

"Yeah, why not?"

The truck roared to life. Ten minutes later, we were in my driveway. Marcus sat in his seat, looking up at the house. That's when I realized this was the first time he'd be coming inside the house since Ethan had died. Marcus waited for me to get out of the car first, and then he followed me up the steps to the door. He watched carefully, almost as if he were afraid of stepping through the door into the kitchen. Like this was a sacred place he wasn't allowed anymore.

"I've never been in here without him," Marcus said. "It doesn't feel real."

I wanted to agree with him, but for some reason, the silence felt more appropriate. Marcus looked over the half-packed boxes and trash bags.

"The donations?" he asked.

I simply nodded.

He wiped at his nose and then turned back to me. "I'm done." He followed me closely, all the way to my room. I wondered silently what he would've done if I hadn't been there, and then I thought about giving him that chance. To spend a few moments alone with his best friend who wasn't his best friend anymore.

"I had some ideas," he said.

"Yeah? What about?"

"Well." He reached into his backpack. "Depends on what you want."

Marcus pulled out this small composition book, the black-and-white marbled kind. His had been colored in, in a few places, and there were obvious signs of wear, notes sticking out. It looked like he'd had to tape the spine to get it to stay together.

"Is that your notebook?"

"One of them. It's where I write down my ideas that aren't fully formed yet."

"Okay, what do you got?" I asked.

"Lots of ideas, actually. I spent a good chunk of last night researching lyrics and how to write them—"

"You're the one who said they're the same as poetry."

"They are and they aren't."

"I hate the way you talk sometimes," I said, taking a seat on the bed next to him, our knees touching for just a brief moment. I hated that I felt that spark. Sure, I'd had a crush on Marcus a few years ago, but I felt like that was something every kid had. Your older sibling's friends always seemed cooler, more mature, more adult. It was easy to fall for them.

"Did you read some of it?" Marcus asked.

"What?"

When I looked up from his notebook, I realized that he was staring at the Emily Dickinson book on my desk.

"Oh, yeah. I read some last night."

"What did you think?"

"Um . . . it was good. I only read a handful, though. I didn't really know where to start."

"It's cool. You can start anywhere."

Marcus seemed genuinely excited about making a song with

me, which should've made me feel good, I suppose, but he'd been so nonchalant about it yesterday. Maybe inspiration had really struck him. I decided to wait to play him the song from last night.

"So what are you thinking for the song?" I asked.

"That depends—what angle do you want to hit it from?"

"I think that depends on you most of all."

"When I was looking things up, people said it never really mattered which came first, lyrics or music."

"I mean, I have some unfinished songs that we could work on," I said.

"Cool."

"Do you mind if I look through that?" I asked, pointing at the notebook.

"Sure."

I took the notebook delicately, scared that it might fall apart in my hands at any moment. I flipped the pages carefully. There was more of what I could only guess was Marcus's poetry, some ideas he'd written down, the words *love song?* written out beneath the words *warm, hands, heartbeat.*

He'd seemed to capture every emotion he humanly could, writing down all the feelings he associated with them. There were lines of poetry he'd written down, some of them rhyming, some of them not. A few had details written down next to them like *upbeat tempo* or *this part of the song should be slowed down I think.*

"Wow, you went all in on this."

"Well, I use the notebook mostly for my own work. But like I said, I did a lot of research last night."

"You probably didn't have to do that much."

"You wanted my help, and I wanted to help. Why wouldn't I try?"

I kept flipping through, until something caught my eye.

You're on the other side of the wall,
And I want to sneak you a kiss.
Yeah, I want to see your face,
I want to touch your hand.

"What's this one?" I asked.

"Oh, um . . ." He snatched the book away quickly, closing it shut. His face was tinted red. "That's nothing."

"Was that a song about your ex?"

"No . . . it isn't about anyone."

"Sorry."

"It's okay." Marcus stood up. "Why don't we get to work, huh?"

"Yeah, sure." I moved to my desk, stepping around Marcus. I tried to hold my hands out, to avoid touching him, but my bed and my desk were so cramped together that it was nearly impossible. A few shakes of my mouse and my computer screen lit up with GarageBand, right where I'd left it the night before.

"Jesus," Marcus said, eyeing the screen. "This is intense."

"It's music."

"How do you keep track of what all this does?"

"Lots and lots of practice. I've been trying to make things for, like, five years, I think. So I'm pretty familiar with everything here."

"Cool."

"Oh, can I show you the song I wrote with your poem?"

Marcus looked confused. "My poem?"

"The one in the book." I picked it up briefly. "In the back."

I typed in my SoundCloud because I wanted to look cool in front of Marcus; I wanted him to see my followers and my songs, and the hits they'd gotten so far. "Ghosts" had climbed above five hundred listens, and over two hundred likes, which was super exciting for me.

"You used my poem?" Marcus took the book, flipping to the back page where the poem was.

I hit play, and the song started. The melody slowly poured in, the guitars and the drums working together to make things feel a little scary. At least, I'd hoped they did. I watched Marcus's face closely, especially when the lyrics came in, in the middle. His eyes went wide and his mouth opened ever so slightly. I thought he was loving it—

Until he reached over and hit pause.

"Take it down," he said.

"Yeah, I—" Then I stopped, realizing what he'd said. "Wait, what?"

"Take the song down, Liam," he repeated more firmly.

"What? Why would I do that?"

"Because you used my words without permission. Those were private."

"They were in the book." I handed him the Dickinson. "I thought it'd be safe."

"Just because I'd jotted them down in the back of a book didn't mean you could just use them."

"I . . . What's the big deal? It's just a poem."

"The big deal is that the poem is about Ethan. Now take the song down. I want to watch you take it down."

"You're being ridiculous, Marcus."

"No, I'm not. Now take it down."

"I'm not going to take it down. I'm really proud of this song."

"Take. It. Down," Marcus repeated.

"No." I could only stare at him, bewildered at what was happening in front of me. In seconds, Marcus had gone from seeming so carefree and excited to work on music with me to being angry. "It's too late. People have already heard it."

"How many people?" he asked.

I peered at the number of listens it'd gotten. "Like more than five hundred."

"Take it down, Liam, or I will."

"You don't know how to take it down," I said.

"I can figure it out."

"It's just a poem, Marcus. What's the big deal?"

"It's a poem I wrote about him for me, and *only* for me. Jesus Christ. I loved him, and that poem is about him, and it's mine. Not yours, mine." Marcus's gaze was so intensely focused on me that I didn't think he'd realized what he'd said.

I loved him.

"What does that mean?"

"What?"

"You said you loved Ethan."

"I did, Liam. As a friend. I loved him as a friend."

"You're lying," I told him. "I can tell."

"You don't know anything Liam," Marcus said. He bent over, picking up his backpack. "Delete the song or I'll report it."

"No, I'm not going to delete it."

"Delete the song," Marcus said, and then he walked out. I listened to the stomp of his feet on the stairs as he made his way to the back door. I heard Mom say something—she must have just gotten home.

I listened as the door to the house slammed again and Marcus's truck came to life outside, the tires squealing as he backed out of the driveway. I heard Mom's heels as she climbed the stairs, heading right for my room.

"What was that all about?" she asked.

"Nothing," I said, looking at the web page for my song.

"Why was Marcus here?"

"We were working on a project."

"He seemed angry when he left," she said.

"Yeah, well . . . teenage mood swings."

"Liam." The way Mom said my name sounded pained, hurt. And I knew that that was what I'd done to her. I'd made her feel this way, and I didn't like it.

I knew that.

That was the worst part.

I knew I was causing so much pain, and yet I couldn't stop myself.

Mom shook her head and left my room. When Dad got home, I could hear the two of them talking. When they were done, Dad appeared in my doorway.

"Up," he said.

"What?"

"I said get up, Liam."

I stood up from my chair, worried about what was going to happen. Then I saw Dad moving toward my computer.

"What are you doing?" I asked him.

Dad reached behind the monitor, pulling the power cord right out of it. Unfortunately for me, I used a huge iMac, so it was that easy to make the computer completely unusable.

"You'll get this back when you've apologized to your mother,"

Dad said, lifting the computer in his arms. "And when you've worked to fix your grades."

"You can't do that!" I shouted.

"I most certainly can. This is a privilege, not a right."

I watched Dad as he walked across the hallway, into his and Mom's room. Their huge walk-in closet opened up and Dad set my monitor carefully inside.

"What about homework? I have papers that I have to do."

"You can use my work computer," he said. "Or you can use the computers at school."

"What about my music?"

"When you learn to respect your mother, you apologize to her, and you get your grades back up, then you'll be allowed to work on your music."

"This isn't fair."

"Yeah, well, as I believe we've already established, life's not fair, Liam."

"I hate this fucking house!" I shouted at the top of my lungs, and I ran back to my room, slamming the door behind me. I half expected Dad to rush in, to fight with me some more, but he didn't.

I also half expected to hear Ethan laughing at me.

What a drama queen.

I heard the footsteps as Dad moved downstairs, and shame filled my body as I realized what I'd done, what I'd said.

Covering my face with my hands, I sat on the edge of my bed, staring at the empty space where my monitor had sat, all the music and tools inside just gone, hidden in my parents' room with no easy way for me to get to them. I hung my head, not proud of the things I'd said or done. That was when I noticed the notebook under my bed.

I picked it up carefully, still worried that it'd fall apart if I so much as breathed on it incorrectly. I was surprised to see that the inside was still the same, still filled with lyrics and ideas, as if I had actually expected it to have changed in the thirty minutes that'd passed since I'd last flipped through.

I loved him.

I read through the words again, reading and rereading them until I felt my eyes go crossed. I needed something to do, after all, since I couldn't make music.

But I also wanted to know what Marcus had meant.

I loved him.

There was another poem, near the back of the notebook.

Things grow old—
Everything does.
But I promise you—
No matter the distance
My heart beats the same as yours
And you make it full.

The pieces all seemed to click in my head at once.

I opened the Emily Dickinson again.

It was right there in front of me.

For you.

Ethan's handwriting.

I loved him.

This was why Ethan was so depressed those weeks before he died.

This was who he loved.

I loved him.

If I'd known this, if I'd known he was hurting, maybe I would've dragged him out of the house that day, whether he liked it or not, and he might still be alive. Maybe then Marcus might still have the boy he loved in his life. Maybe Ethan would've gone to New York with him. Maybe they would've stayed broken up. Maybe they would have reunited in a few years when Ethan traveled there, their love reignited.

So many maybes, so many new timelines, so many new universes created in the span of just a few words.

I gripped Marcus's notebook closer to my chest, tracing the words that he'd written, words that he'd written for my brother. I didn't realize I was crying at first, but my tears fell to the page, staining the blue ink and forcing it to pool around the letters. I felt my grip on this reality slipping, the knowledge that my brother had this secret, one that he never thought to tell me. I cried for Marcus; I cried for his lost love and the future the two of them might've had. I cried for my parents and how awful their only living child had become, how they seemed to have lost both of their kids in a matter of weeks. I cried for Joel and Vanessa, how they'd hurt me, and how I'd hurt them.

I cried for myself, and all the hurt I'd caused, and all the pain I felt.

But most of all, I cried for Ethan because he was no longer here.

after

I opened my eyes the next morning, sitting up in my normal sheets and staring at the normal walls. I saw all these things every single day of my life, but today, they all felt different, unnatural.

I almost got out of bed, prepared to get on with my day like any other, and I realized I didn't have a way to get to school. Then I remembered that it was Saturday, so I wouldn't have to worry about that.

I lay down in bed, pulling my sheets over my head after I plugged my phone back in its charger and tried my best to fall asleep since I'd barely gotten any the night before. Dad had attempted to talk to me, but after getting nothing but silence, he'd left, leaving dinner at my door. I'd eaten, left the plate for him to take, and then closed my door.

Maybe they'd expected to come into my room this morning and find my dead body, or maybe find that I'd hurt myself or something. I was surprised they hadn't taken my door off the hinges as well.

I'd never contemplated taking my own life before. I never felt like I'd had a reason to. But wasn't now the perfect time?

School was awful. I didn't have friends anymore. I didn't have my parents anymore. And Ethan . . .

I still didn't know how to feel about Ethan, and Marcus, and Ethan *and* Marcus.

I couldn't even fault Mom and Dad for wanting their first son back over me. I was nothing but troubled. Queer, angry, I could never give them what they wanted. I remembered Mom talking when I was younger; she said she'd always wanted two boys, and that God had blessed her with us. That was always at the back of my head when I came out to them, when I told them that I didn't feel like a boy, that I didn't mind he or him but that I couldn't be a son.

Perhaps I could have bartered with God, made a trade for my life over Ethan's.

I looked at my wrist, imagining the lines there, tracing them with my thumb. I wondered how easy it would be, to cut into the skin, to let it all out.

I didn't want to die.

Not really.

What I wanted was to disappear. To blink out of existence, to be forgotten by everyone who ever knew me. I didn't want to be here anymore, to have to think, to have to feel.

What was the point anyway? The older I got, the more people would vanish.

If I lived long enough, I'd have to survive the pain of losing Mom and Dad. Anyone else who I ever loved or met, anyone who I shared my life with.

Why not take that potential pain away?

Why not save myself that?

But if I killed myself, it'd only hurt everyone I loved. Mom and Dad would grieve their two children, lost just over a month between each other.

After a while, I climbed out of bed, still only dressed in my underwear, and I walked down to the bathroom across the hall from Ethan's room. This was the bathroom that we shared, and it was also the bathroom for guests to use when Mom and Dad had people over. I'd always wondered why we couldn't each have our own bathrooms instead of having to share. Ethan was always so messy, leaving his things all over the counter when he was done getting ready in the morning, leaving me to put them all away or else they'd just sit there.

I stared at myself in the mirror, taking in the bags under my eyes, the way my hair had gotten a little too long over the last few weeks, how hollow my cheeks looked, and the light scruff on my jawline, as much as any sixteen-year-old could grow after not shaving for two weeks.

I looked awful.

Like a dying baby bird or something.

I peed, then washed my hands and my face, all the while looking for something. I didn't know what exactly I was looking for, just that I'd know it when I saw it.

And I found it in Ethan's drawer.

We each had drawers that had our things in them. Everything that belonged to us besides our toothbrushes. I had my toothpaste for my overly sensitive teeth in there, my deodorant, this skin stuff that Vanessa made me buy at Lush one time that I never actually used, and some body spray.

Ethan's had more. His toothpaste, his cologne, deodorant, body spray, shaving cream, Q-tips, an electric razor that I had to share when I wanted to shave.

That wasn't what I wanted, though.

I wanted his regular razor.

Which I didn't see.

It wasn't in the drawer anywhere. I emptied it out, laying everything out on the counter as I searched, almost as if Ethan had done it himself, and it wasn't there. I put everything back messily and moved to the shower, pulling the curtain away.

There.

Ethan's razor sat in the soap dish, dry.

I stared at it from afar, looking at the hunter-green handle, the sharp angle of the head. He used this razor that was designed so you could snap off the part that had the razors and replace them easier. I guess it was more environmentally friendly or something.

I didn't see any of his replacement blades. Maybe that would've made this whole endeavor easier.

But I grabbed the razor from its place and sat down in the tub the short way, with my legs hanging over the side, staring at it.

Wondering how it all fit together.

I slid the handle off, leaving it by itself, studying the razors. Pressing it against the skin of my thumb, against the grain. It took pressure, not a lot, but sliding it across the blades once or twice tore at the flesh. Not enough to bleed, but enough to come away, to force me to stare in horror at the way my finger looked now. Close up, the skin was so pale, and it'd torn away so easily.

Silently, I wondered how much damage it could do to the rest of me. I stared at the razor, and then at my arm, pressing the plastic and metal to my wrist. But nothing happened.

I pressed again, harder this time, and still, nothing happened. The only pain I felt was from the sting of the plastic head digging so close to my wrist bone. I wanted more, I wanted this to do more, but it wouldn't.

It made sense—when you were cut by a shaving razor, it was supposed to be an accident, a painful accident that would lead you to change the blades or to be more careful next time.

But I wanted the razor to cut me, to shred my skin, to make me bleed. Anything to get this out of me, this feeling, this pain, this . . .

Everything.

I pressed and I pressed, and I felt the sting.

"Ah, fuck!" I dropped the razor, and it clattered against the white acrylic inside the tub. I watched the fresh cut on my wrist as the blood welled up.

"Shit."

I stood up quickly.

Too quickly, almost slipping and falling to the tiled floor, where I'm sure I would've busted my head open, left there for my parents to find me.

I grabbed the roll of toilet paper that sat on the back of the toilet when I recovered, coming to my senses. I tore at a piece, applying more and more pressure. The moment I'd seen the red line appear . . .

It had scared me.

It had filled me with shame and guilt. But above all else, it had filled me with fear.

I sat down on the floor, my skin crawling with goose bumps from the chilled tiles. I felt the sting of the tears come first, the way the salt spilled over my eyes, trailing its way down my cheeks.

"I'm sorry," I whispered to no one. "I'm sorry, I'm sorry, I'm sorry, I'm sorry, I'm sorry, I'm sorry . . ."

I'm sorry," I told him.

"It's okay, dude—" Ethan stopped himself. "Sorry."

"S'okay," I told him. "I know it's hard or whatever."

"I know you don't like being called 'dude.'"

I shrugged. "You get used to it."

Ethan didn't respond. He simply took the roll of toilet paper that sat on the back of the toilet, tearing off a single piece and ripping that into smaller pieces. "I thought Dad was going to teach you how to shave?"

"He was. And he forgot. And I was sick of my face being itchy."

Ethan smiled, focusing on the fresh cuts on my face. "Why didn't you ask me?"

"You were busy."

265

"I could've helped."

"Sorry."

"Pfft." Ethan placed a piece of toilet paper against my cheek. The worst cut, and the last one I'd made before I dropped the razor into the sink, staining the water pink. "You need to be more careful."

"I know."

"You could've seriously hurt yourself."

"I know!" I snapped, but then I leaned back on the counter, letting him place another piece of toilet paper on another cut. "Sorry."

Ethan focused on my face for a few more minutes. Luckily, I'd only gotten to the right side of my face, where I'd managed to do the most damage. Unfortunately, that now meant that one half of my face was covered in small cuts, and the other half was still covered in dark sparse hair that made my jaw itch.

"Do you want me to show you how to do it?"

"Umm . . ." I stared down at him; this was probably one of the few times that I'd ever be able to look down at Ethan. "Sure?"

"Well, I'm not having you go to school looking like that." He smiled at me. "Imagine if people saw you! And they all know you're my brother. It'd be mortifying."

"Shut up." I looked away from him, but I couldn't help but smile at his laugh. "Just show me how."

"Okay, well . . ." Ethan looked at the counter, which was

crowded with things I'd just tossed wherever, trying to figure out if I needed them or not. I'd seen in movies when people finished shaving, they'd put aftershave on their faces. I didn't know what that kind of bottle looked like, and when I googled it, it seemed pretty similar to the cologne bottle that Ethan had, so I still had no idea if I needed it or not.

Then there was this tub of stuff Ethan had that looked like a balm or a salve, but the label was so worn off that I couldn't tell if it was for his face or for his hair. All I knew was that it smelled like strawberries.

"Your first mistake was not using shaving cream." Ethan showed off this blue-and-white bottle that was topped with a nozzle.

"I don't have to when I use the electric razor," I told him.

"These are two very different things." Ethan set the bottle down and turned on the faucet. "First thing I like to do is wet my hands and my face. Then I use the cream."

He patted his face with his damp hand before he squirted shaving cream onto his open palm, rubbing it in circles along his face lightly.

"Here." He moved out of the way of the sink so I could stand there.

I wet my face and sprayed the shaving cream on my hand.

"Too much," Ethan told me. "You don't need a lot. A little goes a long way."

I took some of the shaving cream and rubbed it all along the half of my face that wasn't covered with cuts and toilet paper.

"Good. Now, the trick with the razor is going with the grain."

"What does that mean?"

Ethan shrugged. "No idea, but when Dad taught me how to shave, he said that and then shaved downward, so I guess that's what it means?"

I laughed. "Okay?"

"So it's not too much pressure, but if you don't apply enough you won't get anything. Just press the razor against your skin." Ethan did exactly that. "Make sure the blades are actually on your skin and not just sitting there like they've got nothing to do."

I watched him carefully, trying to take in every detail of what he was doing and how he was doing it. Ethan pressed the razor against his cheek and pulled it down smoothly. When it came away, he rinsed the shaving cream and hair off the razor and went back for another pull.

"You see?"

"I think so." I stared at him, and that made me laugh. "You look like Santa Claus."

"Shut up." Ethan handed the razor to me, smiling under all the foam. "Here, you try it."

I took the razor and tried my best to copy what Ethan had showed me. Pressed against the skin, pulling down.

"Ow!" My hand fell away, and the razor clattered into the sink.

"You okay?"

"Yeah." I put my fingers to my cheek, expecting to see blood when I pulled it away, but instead there was nothing. "It just . . . it hurt?"

Ethan reached into the sink and handed me the razor. "Here, do it again."

"But it hurt!" I whined.

"Do you want to walk around school looking like that?" He motioned to my reflection.

"No . . ." I mumbled, taking the razor back and trying again. Despite the sting of the drag, I kept going. All the way from the top of my cheek to the bottom of my jawline. "Is that better?"

Ethan took my face in his hands, turning it whichever way he wanted to, like I was a doll. "Close. You're not pressing down enough. Here."

He took the razor and pressed it against my cheek, and my heart started to thud in my chest. I knew that Ethan wouldn't hurt me, not on purpose at least, but if he cut my cheek, it wouldn't be the first time he'd hurt me by accident.

"Feel how I'm pressing it?"

"Yeah?"

"And then you drag down. You need to be pressing against your skin the entire time or else you won't catch everything and it'll be uneven."

"Okay," I grumbled.

Honestly, I was just ready for this to all be over.

"Do it again." Ethan leaned against the wall next to the shower, watching me in the mirror. He still looked hilarious with his face covered in shaving cream and this serious look in his eyes.

So I did it again, and when I was finished, I ran the razor under the faucet, looking at Ethan in the mirror.

"Go again."

I did.

And again, and again, and again, until there was only a little bit of shaving cream stuck to the tops of my ears.

"Okay, now let me see."

I turned toward Ethan, letting him inspect my face carefully.

"You did it!"

"I did?" I turned back to the mirror quickly, ignoring the bandaged side of my face to stare at the smooth side.

"You missed a few spots, but you got most of it."

"What do I do now?"

"You can run the razor over it lightly, make sure you clean it all up. You can only say you're done when you've wiped all the shaving cream off your face."

I stared at my reflection, noticing the few streaks of shaving cream left, so I wet the razor again and ran over the spots carefully, keeping my hand lighter than when I'd originally shaved.

"Good!" Ethan stepped in front of me. "Now give me that thing—I've got to finish up here."

I watched him as he shaved his face.

"See, it's not so hard."

"It hurts sometimes," I told him.

"You get used to it."

"You do?"

Ethan turned to me, his mouth still coated in a layer of bubbly white shaving cream. "Not really. I still nick myself every now and then."

"Yeah?"

"Yep, and I'm always worried to shave around my lips. That shit hurts, and it bleeds for a long time."

"It doesn't look fun."

"It's better than looking scraggly and gross."

"Do you want to grow a beard?"

"Maybe one day. When I'm older." Ethan grinned. "It'll make me look more distinguished."

"I don't want a beard," I said.

"Why not?"

"I'm not supposed to have a beard."

"Is that a part of the whole nonbinary thing?" he asked.

I shrugged. "I don't know. None of the people I've seen have beards."

"Where'd you see all these people?"

"Online, in videos and posts and stuff." I tried to tuck into myself, suddenly feeling self-conscious. This was really the most I'd ever talked to someone about gender. With Mom and Dad, I'd simply told them. They'd wanted me to explain more, but I asked them if we could save it for another day. As far as Joel and Vanessa went, I hadn't had the courage to tell them yet.

"Why can't you be nonbinary with a beard?" Ethan looked at me out of the corner of his eye, sparing a glance before he put his attention back on his face.

"I don't think that's allowed," I told him, because I didn't know any other answer to give him.

"Pfft. That's stupid."

"Why?"

"Because you should be able to be however you want."

"Yeah."

"Like there's no one way to be gay or a lesbian or bi or whatever."

I was surprised to hear him say any of those words. When it came to my family, I thought of them and queerness in two separate bubbles, bubbles that never overlapped. It never seemed to me that any of them had the language to talk about queer people.

But apparently Ethan did?

"So why is there only one way to be nonbinary?" He looked

at me while he asked me this question, and suddenly I felt like I was on the spot.

"I don't know."

"Be however you want to be, Liam," he told me. "And don't let anyone tell you that you can't, not even Mom and Dad."

"What about you?" I asked him. "Aren't you telling me how I'm supposed to be whatever I want?"

He caught my sly smile and replied with his own.

Then he finished shaving and ran the razor under hot water for the last time before he wiped his own face with a wet washcloth.

"Anyone ever told you that you're too smart for your own good?"

"No."

"Good." Ethan tossed the washcloth into the dirty clothes hamper. "'Cause you're not."

On his way out of the bathroom, he mussed my hair, and then he was gone, back to his room; and I was still in the bathroom, staring at my face, and the dots of tissue that decorated one side versus the smooth, cleaned skin on the other side.

I liked what I saw.

S chool continued to be a blur.

As we plunged deeper into May, the summer-long freedom that I was aching for was almost close enough to touch, but just far enough away to seem cruel.

I'd tried to find Marcus that Monday, but he wasn't there. I even looked for his truck in the parking lot after the final bell had rung. Maybe he'd beaten me to it, or maybe he'd never been there. I texted him and he didn't reply.

The next day I spotted him in the senior-eating area. I hadn't walked out to him, though. I didn't know what I'd say to him, what I'd ask. Had he and Ethan really dated? Had they been in love? Was Ethan the boy who'd broken his heart? Had Ethan been willing to let Marcus slip away, to allow Marcus to run off to New York without him?

Dad picked me up from school that day, not saying a word. And when I got home, I fished Marcus's notebook out from between my mattress and the box spring. He hadn't asked for it back yet, so I'd wondered if he'd even noticed that it was gone. How hadn't he realized he was missing something like that? Had his mind just slipped completely, or was he allowing me to have it, even for just a short time? I highly doubted that last one.

If I'd been Marcus, I would've wanted this back.

I shouldn't have, but I opened it again, continuing to look through the pages. Everything was so vague, and I knew from firsthand experience that if you hadn't known the two of them were together, you wouldn't have picked up on what Marcus was writing.

Or perhaps I really was just that dense.

Marcus had written about calloused hands, too-long hair that curled at the ends, sharp angles, and blue eyes. All things that reminded me of Ethan when I closed my eyes. Marcus wrote about first kisses and first times, things that I appreciated the light details on because sex involving my brother was the last thing I wanted to read about.

Then there was a page made out of *sorry*s.

Sorry for not fighting back, for not fighting longer. For not being there, for not being able to handle it, for leaving, for forgetting, for mourning and grieving, for praying, for not crying.

I closed the book, unable to read any more. Things made sense to me now, and I finally had answers to my questions.

I wanted to talk to Marcus. I wanted to figure these things out.

I needed to work up the courage first.

I knew that I didn't want to talk to Marcus in front of anyone. He may have been out, but I didn't know how to feel about outing Ethan. He wouldn't deal with the consequences, but still, it was a personal thing to him. A private story between him and Marcus. I didn't even know if he'd told Mom or Dad, and asked them to keep it a secret from me.

So I waited.

I waited the entire day, unable to concentrate in any of my classes, or through the constant reminders that our exams were coming up in just a few weeks.

When the final bell rang, I ran out of the school, past Joel and Vanessa, who'd become so adept at ignoring me that it was almost like they weren't even trying anymore. I pushed past them and my other classmates, desperate to make it to the student parking lot before Marcus.

I needed to talk to him.

I needed answers.

"Watch it, Cooper!" some kid grunted at me as I pushed past him. I didn't even turn around to see who it was, I just kept running toward the parking lot, the May heat making me sweat underneath my sweater.

I should've been wearing something else, something not made of wool that was going to slowly suffocate me, but I could still see the cut on my wrist and I didn't want anyone else to notice it, even if it had faded to a deep pink.

I could rest when I got to Marcus's truck and realized that he wasn't there yet. Now I only needed to wait.

Eventually, I spied Marcus walking in from his usual spot, the lone building near the back of the campus where his last class of the day was held. He kept his head down, nodding and waving to some of his friends as he made his way toward me. He didn't spot me for a long time, but when he did, I could see the expression on his face. One of concern, sadness, maybe even fear.

He didn't say a word, not until he was throwing his bag into the back of the truck.

"What do you want, Liam?"

"I want to talk to you."

"Yeah, well . . . we can't always get what we want. Now get away from my truck."

"Not until you let me talk."

"That's what I'm doing right now." Marcus sighed, bracing himself against the side of his truck. "Did you take that song down?"

I didn't want to answer that question. "My parents took my computer away."

"Isn't there an app for that SoundCloud or whatever? Can't you do it that way?" His tone got deeper, more serious.

"Yeah . . . I just . . . haven't had the time."

"I'm sure it takes two seconds," Marcus said.

"If you talk to me, I'll delete it."

Marcus looked at me and then looked down at the asphalt that coated the parking lot, the white lines crisp from when it'd been repaved over the last summer.

Then he sighed again. "Delete it first."

"How do I know you won't just leave after I do that?"

"How do I know you won't keep the song up after you're done talking to me?" he asked.

"Touché."

I pulled out my phone, scooting closer to Marcus so he could see my screen. I pulled up the app, went to my songs, clicked on the details of "Ghosts," and scrolled down until I hit delete in big red letters. The app asked me to confirm, if I was sure. I wasn't; I didn't want to delete the song, and I knew in the back of my mind that I could just edit out Marcus's lyrics, take them out and repost the song, and everything would be fine. Except for the 1,300 listeners I'd had, who would be confused that a new version of the old song had been uploaded, and all the comments would be gone. People might unfollow me for it.

I didn't want to delete it.

But I knew that I had to.

"There." I showed him the screen. "It's gone."

"Good, now go home."

"You said that you'd talk to me. You promised."

"I didn't promise shit, Liam. Now go away."

"If you don't talk to me"—I hoisted my backpack into my lap and pulled out the worn notebook—"you don't get this back." I showed him the cover, just barely hinting, making sure I was far enough away that he couldn't lunge at me and take it back. Then I'd have nothing.

"Where did you get that?"

"You left it in my room. After you stormed out."

"Give it back."

"No."

"Liam." Marcus moved in my direction. "Give that back to me. That's mine."

"I'll give it back when you answer a few questions I have."

We weren't attracting a crowd, but it was clear that some people were wondering what was going on. They stared at us as they walked toward their cars, muttering something under their breath. I didn't take my eyes off Marcus, though. I wasn't going to let him get the upper hand or surprise me.

"Give that back."

"I will," I told him.

"Liam."

"Please," I begged. "Just answer some questions. Tell me what happened."

Marcus stared at me and then looked away quickly, as if he couldn't stand the idea of looking at me anymore. Then he sighed for a third time, and I knew that I'd won.

"Fine. Not here, though."

"Where do you want to go?"

"Somewhere private. Come on."

I watched him carefully, making sure that he wasn't going to pull a fast one, snatch the notebook out of my hands and run back to his truck. He didn't, though. He stayed in front of me the entire walk we took. It only took me a few seconds to see which direction we were going and to figure out that he was taking me to the dugout. I followed in silence, jumping over the fence with Marcus, walking through the clay-colored dirt behind him, kicking up a trail that dusted my pant legs and shoes.

The dugout was stuffy just like I remembered, and I breathed in dust as I watched Marcus take a seat at the far end.

The problem was that I didn't know how to begin this conversation. How did you ask someone if they were in love with your brother? If they loved each other in a way that you'd never suspected?

"So," Marcus said. "What do you want to know?"

"Everything."

"That's a long story."

"I've got the time."

"Give me my notebook." He held out his hand, and this time I didn't argue with him. I just reached back into my backpack and handed it to him. Marcus took it carefully.

"You said that you were in love with him. Did he love you back?"

Marcus chuckled, then began to shake his head. "I'd think so. We dated for nearly two years."

I didn't know why that surprised me. Now I'd have to think about all their interactions together, every stolen moment, every kiss.

Marcus went on. "Well, if you'd asked Ethan, he would've said we'd been dating since like eighth grade. That was the first time we kissed. But yeah, I got the balls to ask him out two years ago."

"So you were boyfriends," I not so much asked as declared.

"Yeah, we were."

"Did you tell anyone?"

"No. Ethan didn't know if he was ready to be out, and I wanted to respect his decision. He did tell me once that he wanted to come out before prom, though. He wanted to go with me."

"Ethan told me he had this girlfriend who went to a different school."

Marcus actually laughed at that. "And you believed him?"

"I didn't know what else I could believe."

"What did he say about me, when he was calling me his girlfriend?"

"Oh, um . . ." I tried to remember the things that Ethan and I had talked about that night. "That he loved you, and that he wanted to spend the rest of his life with you."

Marcus scoffed. "Well, that was a crock of shit. Your brother was such a liar."

"What do you mean?"

"I mean that he said he wanted to spend the rest of his life with me; he promised me that he'd always be there." Marcus stood up quickly and I backed away. "But it was a lie, Liam. Your brother was a liar."

Marcus reared back, throwing the notebook at the wall. The paper inside exploded like a bomb, floating through the air before settling on the dusty concrete, stained with an orange that would never fully vanish.

"He wasn't a liar," I said. "Ethan wasn't a liar."

"Then tell me why he broke my heart. Tell me why he didn't want to try. Tell me how *always be there* turned into *we'll be too far away.*"

"Ethan loved you."

"Ethan *destroyed* me, Liam."

I saw the tears in his eyes, the way his hands began to shake.

"Why did he tell me that breaking up with me now was best for us both? Why did Ethan do that? Do you have an answer for me? Huh?"

I stepped back as Marcus got closer, his face more red.

"He just wanted what he thought was best for you," I whispered. "That's all Ethan ever wanted."

Marcus acted like he was going to fall to the ground, but instead, he fell to the bench, covering his face with his hands while he wailed loudly. I'd never seen Marcus cry before; this was an entirely new sensation, and I didn't know how to handle it.

"Marcus," I said his name quietly, but he just kept crying.

"He said that he loved me. He said that he loved me and he didn't want me to worry about him after I moved. I begged him to come with me. I begged and begged and said that New York had plenty of schools for him."

He pulled his hands away, wiping at his nose.

"But he just kept saying he had to stay here, stay near his family, that he couldn't go away. And he wanted me to have my own life while I was there. So he ended things."

I took a seat next to Marcus. "It sounds like he wanted to protect you."

"You don't know shit, Liam. Stop acting like you do."

"Okay," I said, rubbing my hands together.

"And I'm a fucking coward who couldn't even go to his funeral, who can't even visit his grave. The boy I loved is dead and I can't even do that for him."

"I haven't been there either."

Marcus stayed hunched forward, his face mostly hidden from me.

"He wouldn't have hated you for it," I said. "Not going to the funeral, not seeing him."

"How do you know?"

"He was my brother. I knew him in ways you didn't. He wasn't into the ceremony of everything. It would've mattered more that you were thinking of him."

Marcus gave a sad laugh, one that broke my heart. "All the time. I'm thinking about him *all the time*. Not that he knows that. He's gone."

"Yeah. He is."

We were both quiet for a long time, and I watched Marcus's body as he hunched over, so much pain that he'd withheld from the world.

"I asked him out in our sophomore year," Marcus said. "He was staying over at my house, and we were talking. I thought he'd fallen asleep, but he hadn't. Neither of us could. We just kept talking and talking, and then he kissed me."

Marcus let out a shuddering breath, as if he were on the verge of losing it all over again.

He probably was.

I felt that way too.

"It wasn't the first time we'd kissed, but those other times, we just kept saying it was practice, it was practice, it was practice. Boys being boys. This time it was different, though, and I said it wasn't practice, I told him it'd never been practice for me. We fell asleep kissing each other, and before we passed out I asked him to be my boyfriend. He said yes."

"I always thought you two were close, but never that close."

Marcus looked my way. "He always thought you'd be the first to figure it out."

"Did my parents know? Or yours?"

"Ethan said that he wanted to come out on his own time, and I wanted to respect that. So I waited and waited. I never minded, though, as long as I got to have him in private. That's all that mattered to me."

"I think that's beautiful," I said.

"You think that because it's not you. I respected his decision; he wasn't ready. Not being able to hold his hand, to kiss him in public, to hold him close to me anywhere but our bedrooms . . . it was hell. But we could have made it through that. I think eventually we would have told everyone. But then NYU accepted me, and it all started to fall apart. We talked for a long time after that, and I noticed he was distant. Finally, I asked him what was wrong. He wanted me to come to his house so we could talk in person. So I did."

"Was that the day that you saw me practicing with him in the yard?" I asked.

Marcus nodded.

"He got so depressed after that."

"Yeah, well, that made two of us. I was a wreck when he ended things. I never wanted to talk to him ever again. I was so angry."

"I'm sure he just wanted what was best for you, Marcus."

"*He* was what was best for me. He was the first person I ever felt like I could be myself around. He never judged me or questioned what kind of shit I liked to read or watch. There were days where we didn't have to talk to each other because our company was enough." Marcus stood up again, pacing to the other end of the dugout. "He was the only boy I think I'll ever love the way I did. And now he's gone."

Marcus's hand wrapped around the chain-link fence that blocked out the rest of the ball field. It rattled under his touch.

"It doesn't matter anymore. Nothing matters. He's gone."

"I'm sorry."

"Why?" Marcus asked with an aggressive tone. "You didn't

kill him; some asshole did. Some monster who didn't even have the fucking balls to stay with him and call the ambulance. Maybe he'd still fucking be here if the world wasn't full of goddamn cowards." Marcus lashed out again, and I could see where the chain-link fence was on the verge of coming unhooked from the top of the dugout.

"Marcus, Marcus." I reached up to him, placing my hand on his shoulder. "Stop it—you're going to break something."

"So what?" Marcus released the fence, taking a step back. "It doesn't matter. It doesn't fucking matter."

I watched him as he sat down again, and I didn't know what else to do, so I began to gather up the papers that'd fallen from his notebook.

"Leave them," he said.

"No, they're yours."

"I don't want them."

When I'd gathered them all together and sandwiched the loose papers between the torn notebook cover, I handed them back to him. "Yes, you do. They're your memories."

Marcus just shook his head and snatched the notebook out of my hand.

"Whatever." Marcus eyed the pages, flipping through them carefully. "I had so much I wanted to say to him, and now it's too late."

"It's never too late," I said, because I thought that sounded like something smart, something that might make this whole situation better.

"It literally couldn't be more late, Liam," Marcus huffed, standing up. "You don't have to be so stupid."

"And you don't have to be so cruel."

"Whatever," he said, walking toward the exit. "Come on— I'll take you home."

I didn't know if I should get in a car with Marcus, but I didn't have another way home, not unless I wanted to wait an extra hour until Dad could get off work to come get me. So I followed him.

The ride was short and quiet, the tense kind of quiet that I wanted to do something about, but when I opened my mouth, I only imagined Marcus telling me to shut up and not talk to him. So I didn't.

I grabbed my bag as we pulled into my driveway.

"Bye . . ." I said.

"Bye."

"Guess I'll see you tomorrow?"

"Yeah, sure."

I climbed out of the truck, and as I made my way up to the door, I heard the sound of a window being rolled down.

"Liam!" Marcus shouted, and I turned back to him, hopeful for even just a split second.

"Yeah?"

"Check under his bed. There's a box where he kept his stuff."

"Do you want it?"

"No." Marcus stared at the wheel. "You keep it. It's yours."

"Are you sure?" I tried to shout, but he was already rolling the window up, putting the truck into reverse and backing down the driveway.

As I watched Marcus race down the road, vanishing from my view, I had the sinking suspicion that we'd come to some kind of silent agreement. That when we saw each other next, we could maybe acknowledge it, but from that point on, we were strangers, nobodies to each other.

I couldn't bring Ethan back. And short of that, there wasn't anything I could do to help Marcus.

He moved to New York the week after he graduated, and I tried so many times to go and see him. I thought about sending him emails, calling him, going to one of his book signings, but aside from buying his collections of poetry and his novels where the stories bore a striking resemblance to a real-life love lost, I never saw Marcus again.

Once I was inside, I went into Ethan's room.

There was a box right where Marcus said it would be.

I got on my knees and dug my hands deep underneath Ethan's bed. It was a mess; there was clothing, socks, and underwear all balled up and thrown down there. Mom and Dad hadn't gotten that far before I'd chased them away.

"Jesus, Ethan, you're so disgusting," I muttered, eventually having to fish my phone out of my pocket to pinpoint the box I was supposed to be looking for.

Eventually, my hands found it. At first glance, it seemed like the kind of box that you might put a gift in, maybe a little bit sturdier. I inspected the top, running my hand along the small inscription that was written in the corner of the lid.

For you.

For Ethan?

I stared at the box, unsure of what to do here exactly. Marcus had essentially given me permission to open it. But did I want that?

Did I have a right to open this?

It wasn't my property, and it was very obvious that Ethan had wanted to keep it a secret, or else he wouldn't have buried it underneath his bed.

This was a secret that he'd wanted to keep.

Was I allowed to know it? I opened it slowly, wary of anything fragile that might be inside.

The box was heavier than I'd thought it might be, and as the lid slid off, I saw that it had been stuffed to the brim with . . . so many things.

There were folded-up pieces of paper, pictures, stubs of movie tickets. There was a postcard with a picture of a flower and a program for some Broadway show.

So it was a gift box, filled with memories.

Memories that had to have been years old at this point, with the way it was so filled. Memories that belonged to Ethan, and to Ethan and Marcus. I took out the envelope at the top, sliding out the letter inside. It didn't seem that old, but based on the creases, I'd guessed that it'd been folded and unfolded many times, read over and over again.

Dear Ethan,

I love you. I'll never get tired of saying that, I know it's cheesy and that you think I'm a big wuss or whatever. I can almost imagine the look on your face. I mean, I'll see the look on your face when you open this, but I can picture it just fine now. The way that your mouth will curl up on the sides before you actually smile, the way your brow is going to furrow and your eyes are going to concentrate.

You'll laugh as you read these words, because you love to laugh too. And I love that about you the most, I think. The list is long, believe me, but that's at the top.

I wanted this gift to be special. I don't know why, it's not like this is the first birthday we've celebrated together. But I wanted it to be something, I wanted to give you lots of things to remember me by. I know it'll be a few more months, and that we have plenty of time, but I wanted you to go ahead and have all these.

I won't write down everything. I tried to pick obvious things. There's the ticket stub from when we went to go see the last Star Wars *movie. I still remember how much you cried when Luke died, and how excited you got when Yoda showed up. You're such a dork, but that's one of the things I love about you the most.*

And there's the postcard that I got in New York when the school took us on that trip. I'm still not over that, eighteen hours total on a cramped bus all for ten hours in one of the coolest cities on the planet. But I spent that entire trip with you, so it was worth it.

There's the Playbill *for* Dear Evan Hansen. *I know that you really wanted to go and see it, and I'm sorry the tickets were so expensive. So I bought this one off eBay, which sounds stupid or whatever, but consider this a gift in advance. One day I'll buy you tickets to go see whatever musical you want to go and see. That's how much I love you, Ethan Cooper, I'm willing to put up with show tunes for you.*

There's a lot in this box, and I want you to discover it all for yourself, so the rest is going to be a surprise. And don't worry, if you don't remember something, or you don't know where it's from, I know how forgetful you are. Hopefully remembering that I gave it to you will be enough.

Happy birthday, Ethan. I love you.

Marcus

It wasn't like my brother was a different person now. But still, this changed things. I couldn't explain how, but it did. And rereading Marcus's words, my heart broke. Because he loved Ethan.

He'd loved my brother.

And he'd lost him.

Below me, I heard the back door open and slam shut again.

"Liam, are you home?"

It was Mom, home from work.

"I'm upstairs," I said. I moved quickly, taking the box with me into my room and sliding it under my bed just as I heard Mom making her way up the stairs. She stared at me as I collapsed on my bed, my backpack in front of me as if I were about to get a book out for studying.

"I've already told your father, but I'm going to your grandmother's to help her with some things."

293

"Okay," I said.

"I'll probably be back late," Mom told me, already walking into her and Dad's room. "You know how she is."

"Yeah."

It was the most normal conversation we'd had since our blowup, and it actually felt good to talk to her. And then I couldn't help but think about Marcus and Ethan, how their last interaction had been a fight, and how Marcus had never gotten the chance to reconcile his feelings with Ethan.

I still had that chance with Mom, but who knew how long I might have it? I couldn't picture a world without my mother; I didn't want to do that. But I never could have pictured a world without Ethan either.

I knew that I had to apologize.

Because one day my chance would be gone.

But knowing what you have to do and actually doing what you need to are two different things, two separate worlds. Mom moved in her room, and she walked out of her room a second later, having changed from her work clothes into a casual T-shirt and jeans.

I followed her downstairs under the guise of getting some water. For weeks now I'd been looking for the opportunity to not make this awkward or painful, but I think I was only ready to make the right move when I accepted that there was no way this was going to happen without any ugliness.

I watched her check herself in the mirror, and then she grabbed the worn-out tennis shoes that she kept by the door, the shoes that she wore whenever she had yard work that she needed to do.

I grabbed my water and prepared to go back up to my room, my chance at an apology gone. I'd sit up in my room, work on my music, and continue to ignore my mother until one day I'd graduate, maybe go to college, have a career of some kind, and never talk to my mother again until it was too late and one of us would be dead.

Was that really how I wanted to live the rest of my life?

Did I want to leave home one day, still having never talked to my mother, when it was too late to seek any kind of resolution, any kind of closure? Was that how I wanted to live?

I knew the answer, just like I always seemed to.

But I didn't know what to do about it.

"Hey, um . . ." I started to say, scared of the words I might say next.

Mom didn't look up; she was still bent over, tying up the laces on her shoes.

"Can I . . ." I couldn't keep my throat from shaking. "Can I come with you?"

Mom tensed; that much was clear from the view I had of her back.

For a moment I thought she might actually tell me that she

wanted to go alone, that she didn't want me with her. But instead she said, "Sure—are you ready to go now?"

"Just let me get my shoes."

"Okay." Mom grabbed her purse. "I'll be in the car."

A few minutes later, I was there with her, nervous about the mere idea of sharing a car ride with my own mother. Which was ridiculous; she was my mother, I shouldn't be worried about being alone with her. But that's where we were. I'd hurt her, and I needed to own up to that.

I just needed to figure out how to do it.

"So . . ." I started to say, trying to think of just the right words to say next. "How was your day?"

"Fine, good," Mom said, adjusting the volume on the radio so the music played softer. "How was yours?"

"Good," I said, and then I thought about it. "Actually, no. It wasn't good."

I turned toward the window, looking out at the houses as we drove out of the neighborhood.

"I'm sorry to hear that."

"Yeah, it hasn't been an easy time."

"Do you want to talk about it?"

"Just, um . . . a lot going on."

"Have you gotten your grades up?" she asked, which wasn't where I wanted this conversation to go, but I didn't think there was any turning around at that point.

"I'm trying."

"I know, sweetheart. I know."

I wanted to talk some more, but Mom ended the conversation there. Not literally, not quite at least, but I could just feel that we were done for now. Another stellar tally for me in the conversation department.

We crossed to the other side of town in silence; all the while I was thinking about the box and everything inside it. I couldn't see why Marcus wouldn't want it back, with those memories, those reminders. And at the same time I could. He'd lost Ethan twice, once in their breakup and once when Ethan died. And there was no coming back from that last one.

Ethan was gone, and we all needed to accept it.

And one day I'd be gone, and so would all the people around me, everyone who I'd loved and cherished. We'd be dead one day, in some form or another.

But didn't that mean that I needed to cherish the time that I had left with them?

Nana hugged me as I walked up the steps of her house. "Well, isn't this a nice surprise."

"Hey, Nana." I hugged her back.

"How's school?"

"It's okay," I told her, lying through my teeth.

"Oh. And you're here to help your mom. You're such a good kid."

"Right," I whispered.

As she dropped her bag off on the counter, Mom asked Nana, "What have you been up to?"

"I've been trying to watch the news, but the television keeps messing up." Nana handed me the remote. "Here, Liam, see if you can fix it."

"Okay." I sat down on the recliner, the one that she'd had for years now, and tried my best to figure out what the "problem" with the television was. For the life of me, I couldn't figure out what she'd done except accidentally put it on mute.

"Is that better?" I asked when the sound returned.

"Oh, yes. Thank you, sweetheart."

"You're welcome."

"Liam, why don't you come outside and help me?" Mom said. "Nana wants a little bit of work done in the garden."

"Yes, ma'am," I said, leaping at the opportunity to not have to hear my grandmother talk at length about people I had never even met.

A half hour later, Mom and I were knee-deep in potting soil and dirt as we cleared spots to put in the dozen or so flowers that Nana had ordered. We hadn't even been able to get away from her because she sat right next to us in her garden chair.

"Hand me those hydrangeas," Mom said.

"Oh, um . . ."

"The blue ones, shaped like balls with tiny petals."

"Right." I picked up the light blue bush of hydrangeas, way heavier than it seemed, and hoisted it over to Mom.

"Thanks." She took out the box cutter in her pocket and sliced the plastic container the flowers sat in, pulling them free and spraying dirt everywhere.

"You know, Liam," Nana started to say, "have I ever told you how hydrangeas came to be my favorite flower?"

Mom and I shot each other a look. I'd heard the story at least a dozen times. "Yeah, Nana."

"Hey," Mom said, "would you mind getting us some water?"

"Well, of course. You two have been working so hard, you'll need something to cool down with." Nana groaned as she got out of her chair, stretching her legs before she tried to march up the steps.

"That'll keep her busy for a bit," Mom said.

"How much longer do you think this'll take?" I asked.

"We have to plant all of those." Mom pointed at the flowers we still had left.

"Jesus."

"You're telling me. But your uncle wouldn't dare to help, your father's busy, and I don't want her to get out here and try to do it herself. You know how she is."

"She's your mother," I said.

"And *your* grandmother." Mom poked me with her gloved hand, and we both began to laugh. It was odd; it was as if the last month and a half hadn't happened, Ethan hadn't died, we hadn't fought, I hadn't broken down in front of her, yelled at her, told her that I essentially hated her and Dad. "Thank you for offering to come."

"It's no big deal. Actually, I was hoping that I could talk to you, just the two of us."

Mom smiled, another moment that felt rare these days. "I thought that's what we were doing."

"Yeah, but, like . . ." It sounded so stupid in my head. I'd just have to copy what I'd done with Marcus; I'd just have to come out and say what I needed to say. "I'm sorry, Mom."

"Liam—"

"No, I'm sorry for the things I said, and for the things I did. I'm sorry for the way I've behaved. I'm sorry for being an awful child."

I didn't want to cry, but I felt my face falling without permission.

"I'm just so tired," I told her. "I'm tired of being this way and I'm tired of my brain being broken and I'm tired, Mommy. I'm tired."

"Liam, honey. Come here." Mom pulled me in closer to her. Despite our height difference, I felt so small next to her, like

I was still five years old and I was running to her because I'd stubbed my toe on the corner of a table.

"I'm sorry, Mom, I'm so sorry."

"I forgive you. It's okay."

"No, it's not. I've been so awful to you and Dad, and I'm so sorry."

"Listen to me, okay?" She took my chin in her hand and pointed my face upward at her. "Just listen."

I nodded carefully.

"I know this hasn't been an easy time for you, Lee. I wish I could've made it simple, but the truth is that your father and I don't have any idea what's going on either. We're still trying to figure out what we're doing."

I let my gaze fall to the grass.

She still couldn't talk about Ethan. She wouldn't be able to for a while after that, but she'd eventually get there.

"And I can't imagine how much harder it's been on you, being so young, when everything's so confusing. I remember when I was your age, I thought I knew how the world worked, thought I had everything figured out. But life isn't that simple. Trust me, I know." She reached up, tucking a strand of hair behind my ear. "I don't blame you for what happened. This entire experience has been hard on us."

"Yeah."

"And I'm not going to lie to you because I think you can

handle it. What you did hurt me, Liam. The things that you said, they hurt me a lot."

I opened my mouth again, but Mom stopped me.

"And I know you're sorry, I know you are. But it's taken me time just like it's taken you time."

"I don't know what's going on in my brain."

"There's probably a lot going on in there." She rubbed the top of my head. "And it's okay."

"I'm sorry."

"I know you are, sweetie. It's okay—we're going to be okay," Mom cooed.

We sat out there for so long, I was beginning to think that Nana had forgotten about us, but we got back to work when she came out with lemonade instead of water. Mom and I finished up the planting an hour and a half later. Nana was insistent that we stay for the dinner she'd started when she went to make us the lemonade. I felt gross, sweaty, and dirty, Mom and I both did, but Nana didn't seem to mind. I think she was just happy for the company.

While Mom and Nana cleaned up in the kitchen, I made my way to the den, to the piano.

I sat down on the bench, lifting the cover and tracing the keys with my fingers. I didn't play anything specific, just what I thought might sound good, and then my fingers found the sound of the last song I'd written, that slow melody that built to a drop. On a piano, there was no drop, just the notes becoming more and more intense as my fingers found their place.

I didn't notice that Mom was there listening until she sat beside me.

I drew my fingers back, prepared to let the notes die.

"No, no, keep playing." She brushed the hair out of her face, and as I saw her profile, the hook of her nose and the shape of her eyes, I truly realized just how much she and Ethan looked alike.

"I was just playing this song I wrote."

"Play it for me?"

"It sounds stupid on piano. It's better on my computer. You don't have to pretend to like it."

"No, I've always liked your music. It's . . . interesting."

I chuckled. "Thanks for the confidence, Mom."

"You know, this was my piano growing up."

"It was?"

"Yep. Your grandmother always thought that a proper young lady would know how to play the piano."

"Okay, Jane Austen."

"I'm not *that* old," Mom said, putting her fingers over the keys. "When you said that you wanted to take lessons, I didn't really know what to think because I'd hated my lessons. Actually hated going to them. Nana and I had a huge fight about it when I was little."

"Was it that big of a deal?"

"No, not at all. But I was thirteen, and everything was a big deal back then." Mom chuckled softly. "I really hated her for a while after that."

"And you stopped playing?"

"No, she made me do it until I graduated from high school. She said when I went to college, I could rebel as much as I wanted." Mom placed her hands in the proper positions and started playing the keys. I recognized the beginning of "Ode to Joy." She missed a few keys, her fingers slipped once or twice, but she wasn't bad. She'd retained a lot.

"You're a lot better than I am," she said when she was through.

"Practice, practice, practice."

"What do you want to do? With your music."

I couldn't tell if this was a conversation that she actually wanted to have, or if she was just humoring me. I wanted to believe that she cared, that our conversation in the garden would be the start of something new.

"I don't know," I said, even though I'd thought about it for years. I knew the answer; I was just embarrassed to say it out loud.

"Sure you do." Mom nudged me with her shoulder.

"I mean . . . I guess an album. That's the obvious goal, right?"

"Right." Mom leaned in, like she was actually paying attention to me and she wanted to know the answers.

"Producing might be cool too, for bigger names. Lots of people get popular that way, make lots of money, get lots of work."

"That'd be cool." She focused back on the keys.

"Yeah, I think so."

"So . . . has something happened between you and Joel and Vanessa?"

My stomach sank once again, and I missed another note as my fingers slipped off the keys. "Yeah."

"Do you want to talk about that?"

"Not really. I mean, there's nothing really to say."

"Why?"

"Because I fucked things up," I said without thinking, and then I double-checked that Nana wasn't around to hear me swearing. "And so did they. Those two things combined mean it's too late."

"Who said it was too late?"

"I did."

"Have you talked it over with them?"

"It wouldn't fix anything."

"I think you aren't giving your friends enough credit," Mom said, watching my fingers on the keys. "Vanessa loves you. And Joel . . . well, you two have been friends for a long time. Just try. People might surprise you."

"I don't know if I believe that."

"Katherine?" Nana called from the kitchen. "Where did you go?"

Mom sighed and buried her face in her hands. "Lord knows what she's gotten herself into."

"Good luck," I told her.

"Oh no." Mom's hand found a place on my shoulder. "You're coming with me. This is part of your punishment."

"Are you serious?"

"Yep, you don't get away with using that tone with me."

"Ugh." I pressed my hands down on the keys, and the piano let out a long sour note. "Fine."

I wanted to tell her so many things. I wanted to tell her about Joel and Vanessa, about Marcus, about Ethan, about the thoughts I'd had, the self-harm, the cut on my wrist, the trouble at school. And in a way, I did. I felt like we'd had those conversations, I felt them in my brain, even though it'd be another few weeks before I told Mom and Dad the truth about why Joel and Vanessa hadn't been around, and how I'd been feeling. The one thing I'd keep to myself was Ethan and Marcus's secret. Because at the end of the day, it wasn't my secret to tell. I'd protect it for as long as I could.

Mom and Dad would come to understand all my feelings during our therapy sessions together and separately, and we'd find a groove again. We'd still have fights every now and then, talk about ways to help one another. Mom would help me get a job for the summer, just to get me out of the house. We'd find a new normal, eventually.

Right now, though, it was just the start, the beginning of the healing, because we had to begin somewhere.

A re you ready to go?" Mom asked.

"Almost—give me a second," I said, lacing up my shoes.

"Okay." She walked off, the sound of her shoes hitting the floor fading into the background as she walked down the stairs.

Today was the day.

We'd talked about this in therapy, both in my sessions with Mom and Dad, and in my solo sessions. And we'd decided on today. Dr. Ross thought that the first time I'd visit Ethan's grave should have some significance. So I'd decided on the day that he should've graduated.

A hot Friday in the second weekend of June.

While his classmates would be walking across the stage, getting their diplomas and taking pictures with one another in the parking lot afterward, the place that Ethan should've been, we'd all be together somewhere else.

I checked over myself in the mirror, flattening out my hair. The length on it was making it curl and stick up in the back. Dad kept telling me the back of my head looked like a duck's ass because he thought he was funnier than he actually was.

I straightened out my shirt and grabbed the pills that sat on top of my dresser. With a visit to the therapist came a diagnosis. She believed that we'd all been struggling with PTSD, mixed with feelings of depression and anxiety. In our own sessions, Dr. Ross had spoken to me about survivor's guilt, how my brain wasn't fully developed yet and would be less equipped to deal with trauma. I'd also gotten brave enough to tell her about most of everything that had happened with Joel and Vanessa, and she didn't really have any advice for that but assured me that it hadn't helped.

I'd also told her about the one attempt at self-harm, which had turned into a bigger thing than I'd expected it to. Dr. Ross wanted to know so many things: what'd happened days before, the things that surrounded me while I did it, what kind of head-space I'd been in. She told me about how grief strikes you so hard that you aren't even sure if you're yourself anymore. We talked at length about where these feelings had come from, and I promised her that I'd regretted it, that I never wanted to do it again, but there were still my thoughts about wanting to disappear, to blink out of existence, and she talked me through those as well.

It was complicated, to say the least.

But I trusted Dr. Ross. It felt easy to tell her these things after just a month, but with two appointments a week, we had plenty of time to get to know each other. She helped me come up with a mental list of things I could do to get me out of that headspace. Listening to music, watching a movie, talking with Mom and Dad.

She'd also given me her direct phone number, just in case of emergencies. The feelings didn't go away instantly. In fact, I dealt with them for years after I stopped seeing Dr. Ross because I moved away. I always kept her words with me.

There was no easy answer, but having someone who said they understood me, who I could actually feel understood me, made all the difference.

When I was convinced that I looked good enough for a visit to Ethan, I reached under my bed and took out the box, the box that Marcus had given him, the one filled to the brim with the pieces of their relationship. I'd been going through it bit by bit, trying to understand some things, living through their memories together. It was so unfair.

Ethan had been a boy in his prime, with his entire life ahead of him and the love of another boy to carry him. And yet it hadn't been enough.

I took out a picture. It was one of the less personal ones, just of Ethan and Marcus together, Ethan's arm around Marcus's shoulder. It looked like it'd been taken at a party, where they were nothing more than childhood best friends, and not boys who dreamed of spending their lives together. I slipped the picture into my pocket and met Mom and Dad downstairs.

Twenty minutes later, we drove through the entrance of the graveyard, the wrought-iron gates casting ominous shadows onto the grass. Ethan's grave was near the back.

Our monument to Ethan wasn't extravagant. Mom and Dad couldn't afford anything like that, and I'm not sure they would have gotten anything more elaborate even if they could have. Ethan had a simple headstone, with spare flowers scattered around, a picture or two. My guess was that this was all left over from when his classmates would visit him.

"Can I do this alone?" I asked Mom and Dad when we reached the end of the road. The way the graveyard was split up, there were different roads that looped around one another, and typically you'd have to get out of your car if you wanted to go to the proper gravesite.

Mom and Dad looked at each other, and then Mom looked at me. "Of course, honey."

"Are you sure, Lee?" Dad asked.

Dad and I'd had our own talk, less personal than the one I'd had with Mom, but I'd still apologized to him for the way I'd behaved.

"Yeah, just for a bit. Then you guys can come if you want." They'd been here before, to see their son. I was the only one coming for the first time. I wanted this moment with my brother.

"Okay." Mom watched as I climbed out of the car. "Call us if you need us. And let us know when you're ready for us to join you."

"I will."

It was still morning, so it was wet and heavy outside with the summer humidity. The dew covered my shoes instantly, not enough for me to feel the wetness, but I could still see the shimmer of the plastic as it grew damp.

I only had to walk a yard or two to Ethan's headstone.

It was there, like it was waiting for me.

ETHAN DAVID COOPER

01/21/2001—03/24/2019

BELOVED SON, BROTHER, AND FRIEND

"Hey," I said, because I didn't know how else to begin this conversation. "It's been a while."

There was no response, though I suppose it would've been more concerning if there had been one.

"I'm sorry for not visiting you. I just . . . I couldn't bring myself to do it."

As much as the therapy had helped, and as much as I appreciated being able to talk about how I was actually feeling about everything, it still hurt standing there, staring down at this marker of him, some of the last evidence that my brother had actually existed.

"I couldn't bring myself to see you again." I didn't want to cry, but I couldn't help myself. "So I'm sorry."

I sniffled, wiping at my nose with my arm.

"And I'm sorry for crying," I said. "And I'm sorry I keep apologizing."

I laughed, and imagined that he was laughing too.

"Oh boy . . . um . . ." Now that I was here, I didn't know what I wanted to say. There was so much to talk to him about, to ask him about. And yet, at the same time, I just wanted to sit here and enjoy the alone time with my brother.

I knelt down slowly, sitting cross-legged, letting the dew wet the back of my pants. I didn't mind, though.

"A lot's happened since . . . since everything," I told him. "Things got bad with Joel and Vanessa. We don't talk anymore. I miss them, but . . . I don't know if I can ever go back to that. Dr. Ross told me the friendship sounded toxic from all ends, and that maybe it was better that it ended. So I don't know. Maybe you were right all along."

Silence.

"Yeah, I suppose things won't really ever go back to normal, huh? You'd be happy, though—today's graduation day. Marcus is walking, getting his diploma. I found out about everything. I wish you'd said something. I wouldn't have told anyone, I promise."

Nothing.

"I understand it, though. Why you didn't want to tell me. All you ever wanted to do was protect people. That was probably my favorite thing about you." I sat there, looking at all the things that decorated the gravesite and noticed that there was a small piece of notebook paper, folded, weighed down by an extinguished candle.

Written on the outside in bold black letters were the words *To the Boy I Loved*.

I smiled, tracing my hands over the note, and for a moment I considered picking it up and reading whatever Marcus had written inside, but then decided against it.

It was private.

These were Marcus's last words to Ethan.

And they should remain between the two of them.

"Here," I said, taking the picture out of my pocket. I picked up the candle, placing it over the note so that no one could see the worn-out paper anymore. I wanted him to have something, a reminder of the happiest time of his life, with the person he loved the most. Besides me, Mom, and Dad, of course.

Someone who was important to him. Maybe he could carry it over with him, if he ever came back. I looked over my shoulder at the car, and Mom and Dad took that as a sign to join me. I picked up one of the dead, ruined flowers that had been left here for Ethan, twirling the dried stem in my fingers.

"I'll come and visit you more often," I told him. "I promise."

And I meant it.

At least once a month, I'd be here to tell Ethan stories. About how I worked hard on my music and managed to release an EP at the end of that year that I was super proud of, how I found new friends my final year of high school, and how I fell in love with one of them. How I gave my everything to that boy and how he broke my heart the summer after we graduated. How I went to college and studied music. It would get harder when I moved—the music scene wasn't huge in North Carolina—so on my last visit to Ethan, I had to tell him it'd be a while, that it would be hard to see him all the way in New York, but that I still carried him in my heart.

That was years away, though.

In that moment, I had the right-now, and that was all that mattered.

We only stayed for another twenty minutes or so. Mom and

Dad both got teary-eyed, but they never outright sobbed or cried. Neither did I. We told him stories, that we missed him, and then we sat there in silence, as if we'd all mutually agreed to take a moment just for Ethan.

When we were done, Mom and Dad stood up.

"I'll be there in a second," I told them both.

"Okay, sweetie." Mom crouched down, kissing my forehead. "Take your time."

"Okay."

I waited until I heard the car door close, and then I let out a long sigh.

It hurt.

It hurt because I missed him so much. I missed my brother more than anything I'd ever missed before. And I knew that I was never going to stop missing him. But I had to learn to live alongside the pain, alongside this missing part of my life that I'd never get back.

With every single day, it'd get easier. That's what Dr. Ross had told me. It might not feel like it, and some days it would be impossible to wake up without missing him.

The important thing was that I did wake up.

I'd remember Ethan. I'd still love him, whether he was here or not. Because he'd always be here with me, no matter what happened. He was a ghost I'd keep with me for the rest of my life.

And wasn't that what death really was? Forgetting.

Could Ethan truly be gone if I never forgot him?

I'd keep remembering him. I'd keep him alive with me.

I'd be fine.

I knew that I would be.

"Bye, Ethan." I waved to the tombstone. "I love you."

Authors Note

There's a common belief among authors that the second book is the hardest book you'll ever write. Personally, I believe it comes from a sense of proving yourself, making sure that you aren't a one-hit wonder, and escaping from underneath a shadow that we create for ourselves.

I was foolish enough to believe that my second book wouldn't be a challenge. I had it written even before my first book was sold; I thought that I was meticulously plotting out a career, that I was ahead of the curve, that I'd be able to prove myself. Then, in 2017, my father was killed.

It was a random thing, a completely normal Sunday afternoon until my sister-in-law ran into my room to tell me that my father was dead on the street outside our home. It's frightening to think that the events of a single hour change your life forever. I never once considered that my father would die before it was his natural time, when he was old with white hair and wrinkles, and we'd have time to say goodbye to each other. There was no goodbye, no waiting for his time to come, no final meaningful conversation that I can reflect on for the rest of my life. The last words we exchanged were about one of our dogs, who was sitting beside me in my room. He had just smiled at her and asked if I'd walked her, and then he said he was going on a jog with my mother.

That was the last conversation I had with my father. It's the last conversation I'll ever have with him. I suppose I have to be grateful that it wasn't some moment out of a movie, where I told him I hated him. Then again, that would've been a lie. I had spats and arguments with my father, but there was never a time when I hated him, and I'm grateful for that.

It was in this experience that my second book changed, though. For me, writing is a form of therapy, an exercise in drawing out my own emotions. Perhaps it's not the healthiest form of self-care, but it works in its own masochistic way. I decided to write about a child losing a father, and all the messy feelings that accompanied my experiences in dealing with everything that happened.

The twist, however, was that I found that narrative impossible to write. I couldn't bring the feelings out of myself; I couldn't make myself write down these incredibly complex thoughts about my father and our relationship. There exist so many drafts of this book that I found utterly impossible to complete; I'm sure the amount stretches into the dozens. There are thousands of words that led me to the place I am today. So, I graciously asked my editors if I could change the father to a brother, and it was in changing this simple detail that I was able to take several steps back from the situation and see it for what it was.

This is still very much a book about my father, and at the same time, it isn't. There are things in this book that happened almost verbatim, like they were stolen out of a diary that I don't have, taken from a history with my family that I might get in trouble over for sharing. Other things are fabricated for the sake of the story. I think that's key for good storytelling. Truth mixed with a good amount of fiction. It keeps things interesting.

This is a book made of truth and fiction, and it's done that way on purpose because it's the only way that I could write it. I know it won't be for everyone, and that used to scare me at first. There's no love story, the main character is a pain in the ass, the friendships are frustrating, and so much of it is bleak. That used to bother me; it used to worry me that no one would want to read it because of these things. But that no longer concerns me. It's not that I don't care about what my readers think of my work, but to me, this book only matters to one person.

Myself.

This is a book I'm extremely proud of. I told the story that I wanted to tell in the way that I wanted to tell it. It's mine, and that's enough for me. I hope that it will be enough for you too.

Acknowledgments

Sometimes it feels like the fact that this book is out there, in your hands, is a miracle. I spent years writing this story, sometimes never connecting with it, rewriting characters and scenes, and at a point, rewriting the entire thing from scratch to change the tense. The process of writing this book was hard and imperfect. There were moments I didn't think I could do it because parts of writing it required hurting myself in ways I don't think I was prepared for. But in all honesty, I don't think I'd want it any other way. For me, this book was therapy, my way to get out my own frustrations about the death of my father, my failed relationships, and my feelings about myself. Perhaps it's too personal on some level. Maybe I shouldn't have put so much of myself into art that will be critiqued. But I believe that some of the best art is personal.

And that's what this book is. This one is for me.

Don't worry though—y'all will get the next one.

I want to say thank you to my best friend Hương, who helped me with so much of this book and also listened to my problems, my issues, and my thoughts, giving me direction when I felt aimless. You have been behind me for every step of this story's journey. I love you.

There are also so many other friends who listened to my complaints when they didn't have to, and who put things into perspective when I was frustrated. People like Sierra, Cam, Adriana, Corey, Kat, Remi, Lily, Pav, Casey, Mark, Kacen, Preeti, Victoria, Sabina, Amber, Fadwa, Camryn, Cody, and Robin. Thank you.

To my agent, Lauren, who kept me in check and believed in this idea: Sometimes it feels like words will never accurately describe how grateful I am to have you as my agent and friend. It's hard to believe that we've worked together for nearly four years, and I hope that we get so many more together. It really feels like I can accomplish anything with someone like you in my corner. Thank you.

To Jeffrey and David, my editors: I'm not sure exactly what to say. You both believed in this book and realized it was the story I needed to tell next. But you both also saw its problems and the walls it hit, and you helped me find a way around them. It feels like I've found a home at Scholastic, and I'm glad that you're there to lead me along. I also want to take the time to thank the people at Scholastic and the I read YA team for their tireless hard work and dedication. And thank you to Sarah Maxwell for lending her amazing talents to my covers, to Maeve Norton for her cover design, to Nina Goffi and Stephanie Yang for their work on *I Wish You All the Best,* and to Jordana Kulak for her kindness and care.

To my readers: Thank you for your endless support.

To Austin and Rachael: Sorry for not thanking you both the first time. Hopefully this makes up for that.

To my father, Glenn, who died in 2017: I hate that you'll never get to see my books for yourself, but maybe that's for the best. I'm not sure you'd like them, but I know you loved me for me, and that's all that matters. Hardly a day goes by where I don't think of you. I miss you; we all do. I wish that you were still here, to be a father-in-law, a grandfather. I can't fix that; I wish I could. But your memory is in these pages, in these words that I've left behind; I've poured you into this book. I suppose that'll have to be enough. I hope so.

And lastly, to my mother Suzanne: I don't know what to say to you. I really don't. I don't know the words to describe how much I love you, how brave I think you are, how scared we both were on the side of the road that night. I think we've seen each other at our worst, and maybe that's how you know that you really love someone, when you've seen their worst. I've watched for the last few years as you've gone through and survived so much. I hope there are no doubts that I love you, that you're one of the most important people in my life. I love you; I love you so much, and I hope that I can keep proving that to you.

About the Author

Born and raised in a small town in North Carolina, **Mason Deaver** is an award-nominated, bestselling author and designer living in Charlotte. Their debut novel, *I Wish You All the Best*, was named a Junior Library Guild selection and an NPR Concierge Book. Besides writing, they're an active fan of horror movies and video games. You can find them online at masondeaverwrites.com.